"Why Are You Staring At Me, Mr. Bowen?"

Grace asked, crossing her arms under her breasts.

Adam was momentarily distracted by the view. "I just realized how pretty you are. I'll have my chauffeur meet us at the gates of the school. We can discuss your plans for the school—and other things."

"What other things?" she asked, a trace of panic in her voice. "Do you want me to resign? I don't think that would be in the best interests of the school. I'm a good administrator, Adam."

"No, Grace, I don't want you to resign." He liked the way she said his name.

"What do you want?" she asked.

"You."

Dear Reader,

I can still remember how excited I was the first time I saw the movie *Gigi*. I loved the song "Thank Heaven for Little Girls..." I loved the costumes, the exotic accents and the young girl who fell in love with the older man. I didn't realize until I was much older what the story was about. To be honest, it didn't sour the romance for me. A part of me wanted to be Gigi and grow up to be a rich man's mistress. But then get him to fall in love with me and make me his wife!

Writing about a woman who fantasizes about being a rich man's mistress was a way to relive those young-girl dreams. Grace Stephens is a little bit like me. She has a rich fantasy life in which she's way more daring than she would be in real life. Adam Bowen has never really noticed shy Grace before he accidentally stumbles across Grace's fantasy story. And realizes that there's more to the school headmistress than he'd previously suspected!

I hope you enjoy *Make-Believe Mistress,* the first of three mistress-themed books I've written for the Desire line. Next month, watch for *Six-Month Mistress,* in which the heroine really does agree to become a wealthy man's mistress, followed by *High-Society Mistress*—an heiress falls for a man who is out to destroy her father's company.

Please stop by my Web site at www.katherinegarbera.com for a behind-the-scenes look into *Make-Believe Mistress,* including the short story "Adam's Mistress."

Happy reading!

Katherine

KATHERINE GARBERA

MAKE-BELIEVE MISTRESS

Silhouette®

Desire

Published by Silhouette Books
America's Publisher of Contemporary Romance

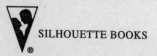

SILHOUETTE BOOKS

®

ISBN-13: 978-0-373-76798-4
ISBN-10:   0-373-76798-6

MAKE-BELIEVE MISTRESS

Visit Silhouette Books at www.eHarlequin.com

Printed in U.S.A.

Recent Books by Katherine Garbera

Silhouette Desire

In Bed with Beauty #1535
Cinderella's Christmas Affair #1546
Let It Ride #1558
Sin City Wedding #1567
Mistress Minded #1587
Rock Me All Night #1672
†His Wedding-Night Wager #1708
†Her High-Stakes Affair #1714
†Their Million-Dollar Night #1720
The Once-A-Mistress Wife #1749
**Make-Believe Mistress #1798

Silhouette Bombshell

Exposed #10
Night Life #23
The Amazon Strain #43
Exclusive #94

*King of Hearts
†What Happens in Vegas…
**The Mistresses

KATHERINE GARBERA

is a strong believer in happily-ever-after. She found her own after meeting her Prince Charming in Fantasyland at Walt Disney World. She's written more than thirty books and has been nominated for career achievement awards from *Romantic Times BOOKreviews* in Series Fantasy and Series Adventure. Katherine recently moved to the Dallas area where she lives with her husband and their two children. Visit Katherine on the Web at www.katherinegarbera.com.

Since I'm now officially an Evelette,
I'd like to say thanks to Janet, Roz, Denise and Lenora
for welcoming me to the gang. And special thanks
to the leader of the Evelette pack...Eve Gaddy!!

One

Adam walked into her office like he owned the place, closing the door behind him and locking it. He brushed his hand along the side of her cheek and tunneled his fingers into her hair, tipping her head back. She shook from the brief contact and bit her lip to keep from asking for more.

Excerpt from "Adam's Mistress" by Stephanie Grace

Grace Stephens found it hard to think when Adam Bowen turned that intense blue-green stare on her. Her pulse beat loudly in the back of her head. Even though she'd rehearsed what she'd say at this meeting a hundred times, in the presence of her secret crush, she couldn't talk.

"Ms. Stephens, I asked you what action you think this board should take," he said.

His voice was deep and slightly gravelly. But it fit him. He was a big man, almost six-foot-two, muscular and totally ripped. She'd never seen him without a healthy tan. However, usually he just glanced over her and moved on. She hadn't anticipated what effect being the center of his attention would have on her.

"Mr. Bowen," she said, sorting through her notes on the table. As soon as she looked away from Adam her concentration returned. She was the headmistress of Tremmel-Bowen Preparatory, a very prestigious school in Plano, Texas, she reminded herself. It was an institution that had long been the breeding ground of powerful world politicians and future captains of industry.

Though lately they'd been in the news more for their scandals.

Get it together, girl.

She cleared her throat and pushed to her feet, wishing her five-foot-two frame was just a little bit taller. She walked to the front of the boardroom where her assistant, Bruce, had set up her laptop and a projector. The vice principal, Jose Martinez, rubbed the back of his neck as she fumbled with her presentation. It wasn't just her job on the line, but the jobs of all her staff. Bruce, Jose and seventy-five teachers and support staff.

"I'm sorry for the delay. I was gathering my thoughts to talk to you and the rest of the board of regents."

She was incredibly nervous about this meeting. The thought of disgrace and unemployment were enough to make her sweat. She refused to go back to the life she'd struggled so hard to escape. The idea was enough to draw her attention back to the matter at hand.

"Tremmel-Bowen has long been the place where diplomats and world leaders send their children for polishing and training to become future world leaders."

"In recent years, that reputation has suffered," Sue-Ellen Hanshaw said. The head of the PTA was a former beauty pageant queen and always made Grace feel like a country mouse. Sue-Ellen's makeup was flawless, her hair salon perfect and her body, of course, in the best shape money could buy.

"I'm aware of that. We've made a lot of changes this year to get the school back on track. But of course, we've had this one minor setback."

"I wouldn't call it minor," Malcolm O'Shea said. As the most active regent on the board, Malcolm had the power to influence the others, to keep the school open.

Of course he wouldn't. It had been his wife—Dawn—whose photo, in a torrid embrace with another teacher, had been splashed across the Internet. Scuttlebutt said that Malcolm and Dawn were currently in mediation preparing for their divorce.

But Adam was still staring at her and his eyes held more than their usual hint of boredom. They held anger, too. She couldn't blame him. After all, she was ultimately responsible for two of her teachers getting caught having sex by her students. She might have been able to manage the students if a picture of the incident hadn't been made public on the school's Web site. Stupid cell-phone cameras.

She felt flames of embarrassment sweep up her neck. Dawn had tried to explain that she'd gotten caught up in the moment and forgotten where she was, but Grace hadn't bought it. She'd kissed her share of guys—okay, maybe fewer than her share—and not once had she forgotten where she was.

Adam cleared his throat and Grace swallowed hard. His eyes held determination; she knew he and the other regents were here to deliver bad news.

The prep school that bore his name, which at one time enjoyed a reputation for being one of the most prestigious in the world, was now mired in scandal and debt. Not at all what his great-grandfather and Angus Tremmel had envisioned when the school was founded more than one hundred years ago. And as headmistress she was ultimately the one to blame. But she had a plan—a plan that had absolutely nothing to do with staring into Adam's deep-blue eyes.

She took a breath and moved to the front of the room. "I want to thank you all for agreeing to this meeting today. I understand your position on closing the school. However, I think once you see the plan that we have ready to implement, you'll give us a second chance."

She skimmed her gaze over the regents, parents and student council, who were also in attendance, keeping a determined and confident smile fixed to her face.

Most of them didn't exactly looked inspired by her speech. And Malcolm didn't look close to even listening to any kind of save-the-school plan.

"We've terminated the contracts of Dawn O'Shea and Vernon Balder. The fraternization policy at the school is very clear. They both understood the reasons for their dismissal. I've made it clear to the staff that there are no exceptions to any of our rules."

"That's a good course of action, but it's not enough to change the board's decision, Ms. Stephens," Malcolm said.

Grace was disappointed by his comment but had expected nothing less. Malcolm had to have been humiliated when the pictures of Dawn were published first on the Internet and then in the local paper. He was out for blood.

"What Malcolm means is that we're also concerned with the school's financial state. As you know, the incident caused many families to withdraw their students and we had to refund tuition, which affected the operating budget for the remainder of the school year," Adam said.

Grace took a deep breath. It was January and the start of the second semester—enrollment had dropped by half. Parents didn't want their future leaders touched by any kind of scandal. She was painfully aware that the school was barely going to cover operating expenses until the school year ended in May.

This was the first conversation she'd had with Adam that had involved more than one- or two-word answers.

"I know that. I've been working with our school accountant and I think we have a plan that will keep us under budget until the end of the year."

"Even if we keep the school open until the end of the semester, we'll be back here discussing the same situation in the fall."

Grace felt her heart drop. Though the board had agreed to this meeting, they'd already made up their minds and there seemed to be nothing she could say to change them. But giving up without a fight wasn't her style.

"I don't agree with that point of view, Mr. Bowen," she said. "Our remaining student body wants to return next year and, together with the student council, we've started an aggressive recruiting campaign."

She'd spent her entire life in pursuit of this one goal—living a proper life and working at this school. She wanted the conservative reputation she now had. She'd wanted to be anything other than the sinful daughter of the Preacher Reverend Stephens.

She forced that to the back of her mind. She definitely wasn't going to dwell on the terribly clichéd fact that her mother had run off with a traveling salesman. Jenny Stephens had left long before Grace had been old enough to ask to go with her, and the reverend had made sure Jenny had little time with Grace thereafter. Although he'd taken her to her mother's funeral after Jenny's death from an aneurysm.

She rubbed the back of her neck and tried to concentrate, but the smell of Adam's cologne distracted her. It was earthy, woodsy, a scent that titillated her senses.

"I'd like the chance to show you our entire presentation before the board votes," she said.

"That's why we're here, Ms. Stephens."

Adam's BlackBerry twittered and he pulled the unit closer to him. His hands were large, his fingers long and his nails nicer looking than hers, which were chewed to the quick.

"Excuse me," Adam said. "I need to see Ms. Stephens outside for a minute."

"Of course, that will give Bruce and me time to set up the presentation for our fiscal reconstruction plan. Will fifteen minutes be enough?" Jose asked.

"Perfect," Adam said.

He gestured for her to lead the way. She was conscious of him walking close behind her until they were outside the boardroom and in the relative privacy of the hallway in the administrative building. He had his hand on the small of her back. She felt the heat of his touch through the layers of her clothing.

She hoped that none of what she'd thought earlier showed on her face. She tried to keep her breathing even and told herself that she was at work, not a place for desire.

"What can I do for you, Mr. Bowen?" she asked, trying to keep her mind on business and not the way his suit jacket fit his broad shoulders.

"I've asked you to call me Adam when we're not in the presence of the other regents," he said.

"It wouldn't be proper," she said, trying not to notice

that the dark-blue shirt he wore made his eyes even brighter and more penetrating than usual.

"And are you always proper, Grace?"

Yes, sadly she was. She nodded. Too bad other members of her staff weren't as vigilant. "I think maybe that's a good thing, considering the problems our school is facing."

He gave her a wry grin. "I need to use your office computer to print an e-mail that I just received and fax back a response."

She led him down the hall to her office. She logged on to her computer and then left him to his work. "I'll be right outside if you need anything."

Adam accessed the Internet and read the e-mail Lana, his assistant, had sent him. Every business had its headaches, but lately running AXIOM was no longer just a fun adventure, especially where Viper was concerned.

Viper had been one of the first bands he'd signed to his label and he felt a sense of loyalty to them. And the last year and a half had been hard on both the band and the label. Lead singer Stevie Taylor's mother had been sick and dying of cancer. Stevie had reacted to his grief by partying harder, and when Stevie drank he got violent. The latest episode involved three staff members at a Paris hotel and the authorities.

Adam rubbed his brow as the list of people he had to talk to lengthened. He needed a conference call with Mitch Hollaran, Stevie's attorney, and Nico DeTrio, AXIOM's attorney.

He picked up the phone and called Lana, giving her specific instructions for dealing with Stevie, who was more trouble than he was worth as far as the bottom line was concerned. But since Viper had made Adam his first million independent of his inheritance, he would put up with more crap from them than any other band he had. He hit the print icon and waited for his document.

As he turned back from the printer, he bumped into Grace's desk. Her office was a decent size, but not really big enough for the large oak desk. Two file folders fell to the floor and papers spilled out of both of them.

He dropped to one knee to pick them up, glancing at the papers for a second. The words *breast* and *mouth* caught his eye, and he pulled that page farther from the folder, reading it. He was surprised to see a very racy story that opened with the boss and secretary engaged in a steamy embrace on an office conference table. It was titled "Adam's Mistress," by Stephanie Grace. Not much of a stretch to conclude that this was Grace's pen name.

But even more intriguing was the fact that "Adam" bore a startling resemblance, both physically and financially, to *him*. And the heroine's name was Grace.

He finished reading that first scene, feeling more than a little aroused by the sexy images he assumed Grace had created. There were almost five pages of first-person fantasy there.

There was a knock on the door. Adam stuffed the

scene back into the folder and covered it with his own papers. "Come in."

Grace stood in the doorway, looking the same as she always had. But for the first time, he really noticed her. Not as a school administrator but as a woman. He couldn't help but see that the silky shirt she wore matched the one her heroine had on. Grace's real blouse was covered with a boxy jacket.

"I'm sorry to interrupt, but Mr. O'Shea is anxious to continue the meeting. Will you need just a few more minutes, or should we reconvene after lunch?"

He was in no hurry to return to the meeting until he had a chance to think about the contents of the folder, but he knew the situation with the school needed to be resolved. Adam followed Grace back down the hall, trying not to dwell on what he'd read. He still saw the professional front she presented to him and the board, but his image of her was shifting. He saw more.

There was a hint of vulnerability in her eyes as she stood at the front of the room, knotting her fingers together as she waited for everyone's attention to return to her. When she spoke her voice was soft but firm. Not loud, not booming. There were layers to this woman he'd never realized were there.

She glanced at the student-council president and her entire demeanor changed. A fire lit in her eyes.

"We're not willing to let one mistake close our school. I've spent the entire weekend meeting with our teachers and staff and then with the student council, and we are all committed to keeping Tremmel-Bowen open. The plan that we've devised is multipronged."

"That's admirable, Ms. Stephens, but—"

"Let her finish, Malcolm," Adam said. "Then we can analyze her plan."

"It's not really my plan, we've all had a say in it."

"Even the PTA?" Malcolm asked.

"We've negotiated a few things with the PTA to get them to buy into this plan, Malcolm."

"Let Sue-Ellen answer for the PTA."

"Yes, we are willing to work with the teachers on this new plan," Sue-Ellen said a bit reluctantly.

Adam leaned back in his chair, listening as Grace talked about fiscal responsibility, community service and new teacher standards and guidelines. She sparkled when she talked about the school, her passion coming to the fore.

"Thank you, Grace," Adam said as she finished her presentation.

"Yes, thank you. I do feel, though, that this is too little too late," Malcolm said.

"Malcolm, why don't we table this discussion until the next meeting?" Adam suggested.

"Sounds like a great idea," Grace said.

Adam called for a vote and Malcolm was the only one to vote against taking a break. Slowly the conference room emptied. Adam held back, waiting until only he and Grace were left in the room.

"I'll see you later," she said, brushing past him and heading back to her office.

Adam knew he should just let her go. That reading the rest of the story he'd found in her office was a bad idea. Pursuing her was an even worse one, but she'd caught his attention. And not just with her passion for getting the school back on track.

She turned to walk out of the room, and for the first time he really watched her. Saw the feminine body beneath the dull clothes that were really too big for her body. Observed the curve of her calf and the sway of her hips. It was pure temptation. Her stride was slow and measured; she moved teasingly with each step she took. She favored skirts that ended at her knee and two-inch heels.

He followed her into her office and found her chatting with her assistant, Bruce.

"Grace, can I have a minute?"

She bit her lower lip and then nodded, closing the door as her assistant left.

"What's the matter?"

She took a seat in one of the guest chairs. As she crossed her legs, the hem of her skirt rose over her knee. He realized for the first time that her legs were bare. Her skin looked satiny smooth.

Adam wasn't sure how to bring up the sexy story he'd read earlier. The fantasy revealed a vulnerability in the woman sitting across from him. One he didn't want anyone else to see.

Her fantasy story was racy, but also very sweet, revealing more of the woman than he'd bet she'd be comfortable knowing she exposed in her writing.

He realized he couldn't confront her with the story he'd slipped into his briefcase. He leaned back in the other guest chair, just watching her. She fidgeted and then a blush stole over her face as she twisted her fingers together. She took a deep breath and glanced away from him.

He'd wanted the meeting to finish so they could officially close the school. His last tie to the lie that was his legacy. But now…now he wanted to linger in town and in her office. Find out how deep those still waters ran in Ms. Grace Stephens.

"I think if we work together we might be able to convince Malcolm and the rest of the board of regents to give you and the school a second chance."

Her eyes widened. "What? I thought you were…"

He smiled at her. "Some new information has come to light and I think that with a little attention both you and the school will benefit."

"It's not like you to be so mysterious, Mr. Bowen."

"No, it's not. We can discuss it over lunch, *Grace*."

She bit her lower lip, tipping her head to one side to study him. "Let's be honest here. Why are you really interested in helping me out?"

Her cheeks were flushed and a tendril of hair that had escaped the clip at the back of her neck curled temptingly against her cheek.

Damned if he wasn't interested in getting to know this woman better. Now that he'd seen those tantalizing glimpses of the woman beneath the very prim headmistress persona.

"Adam? Are you paying attention to anything I've said?"

"Of course," he said. "We can discuss everything over lunch." He repeated the invitation, knowing it sounded more like an order.

He knew there were risks involved—Malcolm was hot on keeping everyone in their very proper place—but Adam wasn't an employee of the school. Just on the advisory board.

He wanted to know more about Grace. And he'd always gotten what he wanted. Sometimes he'd paid a high price for achieving it, but in the end that price had always been worth it. This time, he could oversee getting the school back on track financially—making money was something he was good at. And he could get to know the real Grace Stephens. The one she hid from the world.

"Why are you staring at me?" she asked, crossing her arms under her breasts.

He was momentarily distracted by the view. "I just realized how pretty you are."

She tucked the strand of hair back behind her ear, tilting her head to the side to study him. He wanted her to find whatever it was she was looking for in his face. Some kind of realness or sincerity. The kind of thing that he was never sure that he had.

"Mr. Bowen, are you feeling okay?"

"More than okay. I'll have my chauffeur meet us at the gates of the school. We can discuss your plans for Tremmel-Bowen and other things."

"What other things?" she asked, a trace of panic in her voice. "Do you want me to resign? I don't think that would be in the best interests of the school. I'm a good administrator, Adam."

"No, Grace. I don't want you to resign." He liked the way she said his name. But she only did when she was passionate about something. About the school. When she forgot herself, forgot to be nervous around him.

What would happen if she forgot herself more often?

"What do you want?"

"You."

Two

He swept the papers off her desk and lifted her up onto the polished walnut surface. Slowly, exquisitely he unbuttoned her blouse. Ran his finger down the center of her body, over her sternum and between her ribs. Lingered on her belly button and then stopped at the waistband of her shirt. He slowly retraced the path over her torso. This time his fingers feathered under the demi-cups of her ice-blue bra. A shaft of desire pierced Grace.

Excerpt from "Adam's Mistress" by Stephanie Grace

Grace swallowed hard and reminded herself that he'd just been planning on firing her, so he certainly hadn't meant anything by saying he wanted her. He was probably being clever. What would a sophisticated woman do?

She had no clue. At heart she was a small-town girl who lost herself in her books and imagination. And the attention of a man, the kind of attention that she thought she glimpsed in his eyes—awareness and attraction— that she had absolutely no idea how to handle.

"Grace?"

"Yes?"

"Did I scare you?"

Heck, yes, he'd scared her. But she was the headmistress of this school, a job she intended to keep. So she wasn't going to allow him to see that slight bit of insecurity. "Of course not. You mentioned lunch…"

"That's right, I did, but I don't want you to be afraid of me."

"I'm not afraid of you, Adam." She really wasn't. She was afraid of that inner temptress that her father the preacher had always warned her about. The woman hidden beneath the baggy clothes with the hour glass figure and features that just naturally drew masculine attention. From the time she was thirteen she'd had to repent for this body and now that she had Adam's attention, she wasn't exactly sure what to do with it.

She preferred him to continue to be her secret crush.

"Grace…"

"What?" she asked, not even aware of how long she'd been standing there staring at him.

"Stop it."

"I have no idea what you're talking about," she said,

nibbling on her bottom lip and hoping he wouldn't call her on her lie.

"You're thinking about this too hard. It's just a meal."

There was a tone in his voice that made her feel really ridiculous but she knew she hadn't imagined what he'd said to her. "Then why are you looking at me like I'm on the menu?"

He laughed, a deep masculine sound. "Am I?" he asked, with his charming grin. The one she'd seen him bestow on other women but never on her.

She felt giddy for a second at having captured his attention just by being herself. Not because of her made-for-sin figure, but because of who she was.

Oh, my, she was in over her head. She needed to get this conversation back on to the topic of the school. She shook her head.

"Malcolm wants this place closed down for good, doesn't he?" she asked, desperate to focus on the school and not Adam.

"Can you blame him?" Adam asked. He rose and moved closer to her, leaning one hip against her desk and crossing his legs at the ankles.

It was a totally masculine pose and should have put her at ease, but didn't. There was something measured, calculated in the way he stood there, waiting for her reaction.

She sighed, wondering if he somehow blamed her for the downward spiral of the Vernon-Dawn-Malcolm mess. God knew that she blamed herself for not paying better attention to Dawn and Vernon, but to be honest they'd been two of her best teachers.

"No, I don't. That kind of betrayal would cut so deep. I wish I'd been more observant and realized what was going on."

"What would you have done?" he asked.

"I don't know. Something. Anything to prevent the situation from getting out of hand."

"You can't control the actions of others," he said. There was an emotion in his words that she struggled to define.

"I know. Just think how nice it would be if I could. We wouldn't have to go to lunch to discuss the school, you'd just agree to keep it open."

"Let's go."

She followed him out of her office, trying not to wonder what it would feel like to have his lips on her skin.

He put his hand on the small of her back again. She liked the feeling of his big hand on her. She stumbled a little and he steadied her with his other hand.

"Are you okay?"

"Yes," she said, but inside she wasn't okay. She'd been so careful for her entire life. Made sure to keep her private fantasies carefully tucked away from the reality of the life she carved out for herself.

For the first time she understood that the lines between them were blurry. That they could be crossed. And she wasn't prepared to deal with that.

When would she be? She'd spent the twenty years

since she'd turned thirteen running from her body and the way men reacted to it. When was she going to stop running?

The bell rang while they were in the hallway and she drew Adam to a stop. She wanted him to see the camaraderie between the students. She wanted him to have a glimpse of what he'd be taking from the kids if he didn't vote to let her try to save the school. She wanted him to see that there was something worth saving here.

And nothing could serve as a stronger reminder of what she stood to lose if she let herself contemplate stepping out of the shadows she'd carefully built around herself.

Adam looked down at her as if he wasn't sure what to do with her, and she understood that. She didn't know what to do with herself. She only knew that the life she'd been living wasn't acceptable anymore. It was going to change, because of the situation at the school and because of this man. And if he was interested in her, the way he seemed to be, then she wasn't going to retreat and let this moment pass her by.

Adam had his driver take them to a local chain restaurant and soon was seated across from Grace in a booth.

Something had changed in her demeanor since they'd left her office, but he couldn't put his finger on it. She was starting to relax around him. She still had a barrier in place around her, a formality that she didn't drop, but he could tell she was trying to be friendlier.

"What should I do differently to win over the board members?" she asked after taking a delicate sip of her water.

"Nothing. Most of them are tired of the problems that the school has," he said bluntly.

"Well that was honest." She entwined her long fingers together on the table. He wanted to reach out and touch her, rub his thumb over her knuckles. But he didn't.

"I'm not going to get a chance if Malcolm has anything to say about it."

"You're right about that. But I can override the board's decision or possibly table the formal vote until the end of the school year.

"Your plan has a lot of merit on its own. The board of regents will only be swayed by action and results. I'll be happy to help you implement the changes personally. I think that will be enough to convince the board to give you some extra time."

She flushed as she stared at him. He wanted to know more about what made her tick. Why hadn't he paid attention to Grace before now? "You'd do that?"

She made him feel like a better man than he really was. Maybe it was the knowledge that he was only sitting across from her because she'd aroused his interest with her fictional story about being his mistress. There was something in her eyes that made him feel…well, not empty the way he usually did.

"I don't say things I don't mean."

"I'd heard that about you," she said. "That you don't tolerate lies."

"That's right. I don't," he said, not willing to talk about why. "What else have you heard?"

Not all of the stories that circulated about him were nice. In business, he was ruthless.

"That's all," she said, smiling at him.

He caught his breath as her entire visage changed. Grace Stephens was a stunning beauty when she smiled. A goodness shone through in that smile.

"What have you heard about me?" she asked, her voice suddenly shy.

Not much really. Commendations from parents and students prior to the incident but nothing personal about her. "I've heard very little about the woman behind the headmistress role, but I'd say that you are a woman of hidden depths and passions and that one day some lucky man is going to unlock those secrets."

She tipped her head to the side. "I'm getting a glimpse of that charm of yours."

He was a bit offended that she thought so little of his compliment. "I'm not flirting with you, Grace. Don't belittle the both of us by asking for honesty and then reacting as if it were a lie."

She flushed. "I'm sorry. Anything too close to the truth unsettles me."

"Why?"

She shrugged and looked away from him.

"Look at me, Grace."

She lifted her head, her gaze meeting his squarely. A tendril of her hair had escaped the barrette she'd used to clip it at the back of her neck.

"Why?" he asked again.

"Because I'm afraid of that kind of truth, Adam. I'm not sure how to act around you. You've never looked at me this way before."

"I'm looking now," he said.

"Yes, you are, and I'm not sure why."

He knew that he should come clean and tell her he'd found her erotic story, but his gut said she'd shut him out and he'd never see this Grace Stephens again. Instead he captured her hand, tracing his finger over her fragile wrist and the veins running under her pale skin.

"Does there have to be a reason?"

"I guess not. But I'm sure there is one."

"You're passionate about your students and your school, Grace. There's something different about you when you're defending them, fighting for them."

She licked her lips and he tracked the movement, realizing she didn't wear lipstick. Her mouth was lush, her top lip bow-shaped and the lower one fuller. He wanted to draw her across the table and taste her. To see how she'd react to a kiss. How long would it take to shatter her composure?

"I just know how hard it can be to lose your school at that age. To have to move to a new place."

"Personal experience?"

"Yes."

"I had the feeling that you were practically rooted to Texas."

"I am. I've always wanted to find a place where I fit in and put down roots and I found that at Tremmel-Bowen."

"You didn't grow up in Plano?" he asked, realizing how little he knew about her. It made him feel a little ashamed that they'd known each other for more than three years and he'd never paid any attention to her before this moment.

"No. I didn't."

There was a quiet note in her voice that made him realize there was more to her past than she'd probably want to tell him. "Where'd you grow up?"

"West Texas."

"What city?"

"Why does this matter? I'd rather discuss the school—"

"I give you my word that I'll step in and delay the vote. There's nothing left to discuss about the prep school. I'd rather talk about you," he said.

"Is that the only reason you're willing to help me convince the board to keep the school open? A personal interest in me?"

He was a smart man and knew there wasn't a good answer to this question. But he realized he'd pushed too hard and too personally for her. "No, of course not."

Grace didn't want to talk about herself. Men rarely wanted to know about her. She had no idea what she'd say. She stunk at making small talk and if they weren't going to talk about the school then she was going to have to be sparkling or interesting and, frankly, she didn't think she had that in her.

Luckily their food arrived and she gave it more attention than it deserved. She closed her eyes and offered a brief prayer of thanks for the food. Some of the preacher's teachings she'd never been able to shed.

Okay, none of his teachings, but she didn't like to dwell on the fact that her father was still controlling her behavior years after she'd left him behind.

She tried not to be nervous as their lunch progressed and Adam coaxed the conversation through a lot of different topics. She was surprised by how much he revealed about himself. He didn't seem to have the barriers she always kept in place between herself and everyone else.

She felt a twinge of embarrassment at how professionally he was now behaving toward her. Had she completely misread his interest earlier?

She tucked a strand of hair back toward her clip while the waitress cleared their plates and Adam reached over to capture her hand in his.

"Isn't this cozy?" Sue-Ellen Hanshaw asked as she approached their table.

Grace jerked her hand from Adam's and tried to remind herself that they weren't doing anything untoward. "Adam was giving me some input into the presentation I made earlier."

"I'm sure he was."

"Can we help you with something?" Adam asked.

"I hope you can help get our school back on track," she said. "My son has a year and half left at Tremmel-Bowen and I'd hate to have to pull him out before he can graduate."

"We all want to avoid that situation," Grace said. "I'd love to talk to you and get your input."

"Adam, will you be helping Grace?"

"Not that Grace needs my help, but yes, I'm going to be an active part of the school community until the end of the year."

"I'll be happy to serve on a committee with both of you."

Grace had absolutely no idea how this had happened. She didn't work well in groups. There was no way she wanted both Adam and Sue-Ellen in her office on a regular basis.

"We can work out the details of our committee after the board meets this afternoon," Adam replied.

"I'll look forward to it," Sue-Ellen said and walked away.

Grace glared after her, hating the fact that Sue-Ellen had bullied her way onto a committee that Grace wasn't even sure she wanted to be a part of. If she was on a committee with Sue-Ellen, she'd have a hard time holding her tongue and being the nice little headmistress she was supposed to be. Of all the parents she dealt with, Sue-Ellen was the one who pushed her buttons.

Sue-Ellen glanced back over her shoulder with a smug half-smile. Grace had the feeling Sue-Ellen knew exactly what she did to her.

"Will you do something for me?" Adam asked.

"In return for your help at the school?" She didn't want to say no since he was doing her a huge favor but she'd learned a long time ago not to agree to something without hearing all the details first.

"No. I'm going to help you without you being in my debt."

He seemed a little offended that she'd thought she'd have to pay him for being nice to her. But he was a savvy businessman, and she knew he didn't just donate his time to help anyone out. Even the school that was his family's legacy.

"Then why?"

"Curiosity," he said.

"What do you want me to do?" she asked after a few seconds.

"Have dinner with me," he said.

Dinner with Adam Bowen…oh, my God. She wanted to say yes. She wanted to run and hide at the same time. Her resolution to change herself and not wait for her life to change around her was still so new that she had a moment's thought that she'd just forget about it and sink back into her old life. After all, it was Monday night and she didn't have TiVo. She'd miss her favorite television show.

This was it, she thought, glancing up at him.

"You're staring at me," he said.

She blinked and realized she had been. Just looking at that perfectly formed mouth. Wondering for the millionth time what it would feel like pressed to hers. "Am I?"

He quirked one eyebrow at her. She fought to keep her expression serene. To somehow keep him from guessing that he had any effect on her. But she knew

that he was used to being around much more sophisticated women and a small-town girl from west Texas
was going to be no match for him.

"Yes, you are," he said.

"You're a very attractive man."

"I can't believe you're just noticing," he said.

Startled she had to laugh. "You aren't going to deny
it?"

"Women seem to find the arrangement of my
features pleasing."

She shook her head. An innate charm imbued everything he did and said. She wondered if it stemmed from
his childhood. She knew he was the pampered son of
older parents. And her own childhood had been very
different. Was that the key to adult success?

"I wish I had your confidence," she said before she
could stop the words. She'd gone to school this morning
knowing she was going to have to fight to keep her
career going, never imagining that she'd find herself in
a different relationship with a man she'd fantasized
about for a long time.

"Have dinner with me and I'll teach you how to get
it."

She nodded, unable to say more. This was a fantasy
come true. So why did she feel as if she were about to
start something more potentially scandalous than the
mess she was already in?

Three

Grace needed more of Adam. She wanted more. Her heart beat so swiftly and loudly she was sure he could hear it. She scraped her fingernails lightly down his upper body. He groaned, the sound rumbling up from his chest. He leaned back, bracing himself on his elbows.

And let her explore. This was different than the hurried couplings she'd had with boyfriends in the past. Encounters that had happened in the dark and were over almost before they'd begun.

"Last chance to stop before we go too far, Grace."

Excerpt from "Adam's Mistress" by Stephanie Grace

Adam paid the check and escorted Grace out of the restaurant. He wasn't sure what had happened in there.

Seduction for him was a well-thought-out game and caressing her in the middle of a restaurant had not been his intent.

He put his hand on the small of her back seemingly for the courtesy the gesture afforded, but he acknowledged to himself that he wanted to touch her. He wanted to pull her into his arms and feel her curves nestled against him.

He wanted to kiss her, He wanted to take all the time he wanted to explore her. To figure out the mysterious depths that he sensed were hidden inside her.

He didn't want to go back to the school and drop her off. He didn't want to spend the afternoon in meetings with Malcolm, who was out for revenge and wanted to close the school and then sell it. He didn't want…to leave her.

He liked the quietness she brought to him. The way she really listened when he talked. And the shyness that he had been able to coax her into forgetting while they'd been eating. He also liked her honesty. She wasn't pretending to be someone else or hiding from the mess the school was in.

Lies were something he simply couldn't tolerate, even well-meaning ones, and with Grace he got the impression that she was as honest as the day was long. Though she didn't see herself the same way he did.

He loved her hair and wanted to see it falling around her shoulders instead of clasped at the back of her neck. He seated her in his car, a black Ferrari 599 GTB Fiorano, and walked around to the driver's side.

She fussed with her hair as he started the car.

"What are you doing?"

She glanced over at him, her head tipped to one side. But her hands stayed at the back of her neck. "My hair is a little wild and not very professional."

He could think of no woman who embodied professionalism more than Grace. He captured her wrist and pulled her hands free of her hair. The thick brown length of it spilled around her shoulders. She watched him with wide eyes, clearly waiting to see what he'd do next.

"It's not the hair that makes you professional." She had no idea how upstanding she seemed. He'd never even glanced past the surface of who she was until he'd seen her secret fantasies written on the page. To be honest, a big part of the reason was that she gave the impression of being a no-nonsense, by-the-book administrator.

"Easily said by a man. You have no idea what it's like to be in a room full of perfectly coiffed, straight-haired women and be the only one with this hair," she said, gesturing to her head.

"Does putting it up make you more confident?" he asked. There was a sparkle in her eyes that he thought might be temper. But he knew she wouldn't lose it with him. He was coming to know Grace better than he suspected she wanted him to. The fact of the matter was, Grace needed him to help save her school so she wouldn't tell him off no matter how much he ticked her off.

She shrugged, and he knew that he'd stumbled onto something more than a hairstyle choice. She glanced out the window as he turned on the car. He didn't put the car in gear, only turned on the air conditioning so they didn't roast while they continued the conversation.

Which, it seemed, had stalled. She wasn't going to say anything else and probably expected him to behave in a polite, gentlemanly fashion and let the subject drop. But this woman had written about him in a way that no other woman ever had. On page, she'd made him seem to be a hero. And Adam Bowen had never been anyone's hero.

"Grace…" he said, softly, reaching over to stroke her face. Her skin was the softest he'd ever touched.

She flinched away from him. "Don't, Adam. We can't."

She was right. With the intense public scrutiny of the school, the last thing he should be thinking about was Grace and himself alone. But his mind was consumed with images of the two of them.

He was careful to keep a barrier between himself and other people because he knew he'd always move on. Moving on was the way he survived, something he'd learned the hard way after the death of his parents. He remembered standing in the foyer of that big empty house that had always been filled with their presence and realizing he was all alone. Their deaths when his father's twin-engine Cessna crashed had rocked his world.

But even then he hadn't realized how truly alone he was.

She touched his hand, rubbing her finger over the back of his knuckles and making him realize how soft and small she was compared to him.

"It's not like we even know each other," she said.

"I want to change that. After all, you oversee one of my investment properties."

"Investment property? I thought the school was your family's legacy."

"It's a Bowen legacy, but I view it more from a financial angle," he said in a way that didn't invite more questions.

"And if I don't pull it out of trouble, you're going to lose money—that's your main concern?"

He took her chin in his hand, moving her head up so that their eyes met. He waited a full minute before saying anything to her. Making sure she realized that he was not just using practiced lines to charm her.

"No, Grace. Because you are the kind of woman who makes a man realize there's more to life than investments."

"I am not. Why would you think that?"

"The passion you have for Tremmel-Bowen."

"I've always had it, and you've never noticed me before today."

She had a point, but he wasn't going to mention the story he'd read…"Adam's Mistress." He wanted her to reveal it to him. "It's the way you defended the school and the students."

She took his wrist in both of her hands and tried to move his hand from her face. He let her push him away, his fingers caressing her skin as he dropped his hand to his lap.

When he reached for her again, to tuck a strand of

hair behind her ear, she shifted in the seat and gave him a hard stare.

"I'm warning you."

"Warning me?"

"Yes. This kind of behavior and comments like you just made—that's what I was talking about. Do you think I've never glanced in a mirror and seen myself? I know exactly the type of woman you usually have on your arm."

"I don't have a type," he said. He really didn't. He liked all women no matter what their shape or style. He liked that their bodies were different than his. The feminine grace they used when they moved. The way they really got to the heart of the matter. Just as Grace was doing now, though it was making him uncomfortable. Hell, he thought, he even liked that with Grace. Liked the way she didn't pretend that this was something casual.

"Yeah, right," she said. "I think it's time we returned to the school."

He wondered if she'd sound so sure if she knew the thoughts that prim, school-headmistress tone gave him. He wanted to argue with her, get her to admit he didn't have a type. But there would be time for that later. Tonight.

The problems she'd left behind when she'd gone to lunch with Adam waited for her when she returned. Sue-Ellen had set up an appointment for the next morning. She was gathering the PTA troops and would be bringing other parents who wanted to take an active part in reshaping the school.

Grace had the beginnings of a headache, no doubt brought on by the pressure of trying to convince the board not to close the school. But she thought the intensity that Adam had shown her was also a part of it. She'd wanted him for a long time and now it seemed he was finally noticing her as a woman.

Why?

She sighed and searched around for the budget file that Jose had made notes on.

"Bruce, have you seen my budget file?" she called out the door.

"I put it on the corner of your desk before we left for the meeting," her assistant replied.

Grace went back to her desk and picked up a pile of folders, suddenly remembering that she'd put a story she'd meant to enter in a romance writing contest in a similar folder.

Oh, my God.

Frantic, she started searching through all the folders, not finding the budget report or her story "Adam's Mistress."

Oh, this was so not good. She had absolutely no excuse to have printed the document out here at work, but her printer at home was almost eight years old and it was difficult to find printer ink for it. Currently, she was out.

There was a knock on the door and she glanced up. Jose stood there with a folder in his hand. A folder that was identical to…well, every other folder in her office, since they purchased folders in bulk.

Calm down, Grace.

"Got a minute?"

"Sure," she said, amazed that her voice sounded so calm and serene when inside she was ready to scream.

"I grabbed the budget report to double-check over lunch. I think we need to reevaluate the funds we have."

She was partially relieved that Jose was holding the budget and not her story. "Please tell me we have more money than we thought."

"I wish I could."

She sank down in her chair and gestured for Jose to come farther into the room. "I think we're going to need fifty thousand to make it until the end of the school year."

"That's a lot of car washes," she said. The school had never held many fundraisers. They had a golf tournament every year in the fall to raise funds. But parents and alumni had already contributed to that.

"The kids are willing to participate to some extent, but the one thing we haven't slipped on is our academic excellence."

She understood what Jose was saying. If they asked the students to start participating in a variety of fundraising activities, it would distract them from their studies.

"I have a meeting tomorrow morning with Sue-Ellen. I think the parents will be a great resource for this. Jose, will you please call our alumni president and see if he's available tomorrow at ten?"

"Yes."

"Thanks," she said. As Jose got up and left her office, she sank back into the chair. The next few months were going to be difficult. And she had to find that story she'd printed out.

She didn't need the additional worry that a student would find it. Or worse, Sue-Ellen or Malcolm.

Oh, no. What if Adam had found it?

Was that why he'd taken her to lunch and said he'd help her with the school? Was he setting her up for a private meeting where he'd tell Malcolm about the story and fire her?

She had no time to dwell on that possibility as she spent the afternoon meeting with individual board members. Meetings that Adam had set up for her. The support she garnered was worth the time she spent with them.

The afternoon went by quickly. She had a small break and searched every inch of her office but couldn't find her story. Jose e-mailed her his ideas for their fund shortage, and they were all really good.

"Grace, Dawn O'Shea called while you were in a meeting. She wants to talk to you about possibly getting her job back." Bruce hovered in her doorway uncertainly.

"I can't talk to her today," Grace said. She felt sorry for Dawn, losing her job and her husband. But Dawn's actions had greatly hurt the school, and saving Tremmel-Bowen was Grace's priority.

"I told her you'd call next week."

"Thanks."

Bruce left at six. Grace researched fundraising ideas on the Internet and sent a few links to Jose and Sue-Ellen. She glanced up from her computer at seven-thirty when she heard voices in the outer office. Her head ached at the thought of how much work she still had to do.

The missing story scared her. It had the potential to put all the work she'd done today to save the school to waste. At least she hadn't put her real name on it as the author. But the characters' names—Adam and Grace— were pretty damning. She'd have to change those before she submitted it anywhere. *If* she submitted it.

She knew her assistant would rush back to help her if she called him. But she didn't exactly want Bruce searching her office for that file folder.

"Grace? Got a minute?"

Adam stood in her doorway with Malcolm just behind him. The smile of welcome froze on her face as she noted the file folder held loosely in his hands.

The sinking feeling in her stomach grew as she waited for Malcolm or Adam to speak. She was a nervous wreck and she hated that. This was her domain. The one place in the world that she'd found where she really fit.

"Good evening, gentlemen."

"Ms. Stephens, do you have time to discuss your financial plan with me now?" Malcolm asked.

She wanted to say no. But she wasn't going to turn away from the olive branch that Malcolm offered. All day long she'd heard from other board members that the decision to keep the school open had to be unanimous, so if Malcolm wasn't on board by the end of the school year, Tremmel-Bowen would be closed.

"Sure. I was just about to order some dinner, can I get something for you both?"

"We won't be that long. We can go down to the conference room so we'll have more room."

Grace followed Malcolm down the hall. She empathized with him. She would want to shut down the school as well if she were in Malcolm's shoes. *Betrayal.* It was one thing she understood better than most.

Adam dropped behind to speak to the night-maintenance supervisor and Grace found herself alone with Malcolm. She explained the shortage error they'd just found and then spent forty-five minutes arguing over the tiniest details in the budget. Grace was careful to keep her temper, but she was beginning to believe it was going to be impossible to convince Malcolm to give the school a reprieve.

In the back of her mind was the fear that all the work that she and Adam had done today would be undone by her story surfacing somewhere. She thought of all the people who'd been in and out of her office throughout the day. She'd had the student council representatives in there and, to be honest, she would be even more horrified if one of them had found the folder than if Adam had.

"Ms. Stephens, if you aren't going to pay attention you're just wasting our time."

"I am paying attention. I don't see this as a waste of time."

"I do," he said. She felt the noose tighten and realized that Malcolm might have given in until the end of semester but beyond that he wasn't vested in seeing the school survive.

She reached across the table and touched the back of his hand. He glanced up at her. "Yes?"

"What can I say to you?"

He didn't pretend not to understand her. "*Nothing.* I'm sorry, Grace. I have a lot of respect for you personally but I can't get around the fact that this school needs to be closed."

"You know that knot you have in the pit of your stomach?" she asked, waiting only for his nod.

"That's what you are going to give to the kids. Some of them don't make friends easily. Some of them have their whole life planned with this school, with this education. And no matter that we're in the red financially or that we've had an unfortunate scandal—educationally, we're still top-rated."

"And your point is?"

"That we'll be betraying the trust those students put in this institution. And I know that someone who understands betrayal wouldn't want to do that to anyone, especially not teenagers who are already struggling just to grow up."

Malcolm leaned back in his chair, studying her with an impenetrable gaze. He gathered his papers and put them into his briefcase. "You make a good point, Grace. And I'll consider what you've said until the end of the semester when the board meets again."

She said nothing as the older man left her alone in the boardroom. But she knew she'd scored a victory. A temporary one, a small battle, but still she'd convinced him to give her until the end of the school year to make some significant changes.

And if she didn't find her file folder, it could all be for nothing.

She frowned, thinking of what she had to accomplish. The short time frame she had to accomplish it made her want to scream.

Someone brushed her fingers aside and she glanced over her shoulder to see Adam standing there.

He massaged her shoulders and the tension of the day started to recede. Not totally of course. "Malcolm mentioned he was giving you until the end of the semester to prove the school should be left open."

"Yes, he agreed to that. Thank you, Adam. For arranging all those meetings and for standing behind me. I don't think the board would have given me a chance without that."

She tried to keep her mind on the school. It was the most important thing in her life. But a part of her stared up at Adam and wondered if he'd somehow found the seeds to shut down her school anyway. If he was toying with her because…why? From what she'd seen of him, he wasn't a cruel man.

"No problem. Everyone agrees that if anyone can turn the school around it's you," he said.

"Why do they believe that?" she asked, hating the weakness that question revealed. But tonight, she was a little overwhelmed. Maybe she'd bitten off more than she could chew. Maybe she should have taken the out the board had given her. She could have walked away from the school with a nice recommendation and gotten another job.

"Because you have this inner strength that makes everyone around you realize that you won't settle for anything other than excellence."

She wished she felt that what he'd said was true. But inside she feared she was a fraud. That the fear of having to look for another job, the fear of having to go to some new place and try to fit in had in large part motivated her to save Tremmel-Bowen.

"I'm not that woman," she said.

"Yes, you are," Adam said, using his hands on her shoulders to turn her around and draw her to her feet.

"I don't feel like it."

"You will tomorrow."

"What's going to change between now and then?"

"I'm going to make you dinner and convince you of the faith I have in you."

"We can't. I thought about it this afternoon, you know we can't have dinner together."

"We both have to eat," he said.

She shook her head. If she wanted to save the school, she needed to stay focused on the school and not let Adam distract her. "Our being seen together is too risky. I don't want to chance it."

"Dinner isn't a torrid affair."

"I know that."

"How about if I cook for you?"

"You can cook?"

He quirked one eyebrow at her and gave her a half smile that she felt all the way to her toes. "Yes, ma'am."

She gave her unspoken consent by following him out the door. Already she felt lighter, not as tired, just at the thought of spending more time with him. Adam really was a one-of-a-kind guy. The kind of man worthy of a woman who wasn't always pretending to be someone she wasn't.

Her secrets felt like a heavy burden. And Adam might actually be privy to one that she wanted to keep very private. Going to dinner at his house would give her an opportunity to fish around and see if he'd found "Adam's Mistress" on her desk.

Four

She knew she should tell him to leave, that her job was at stake, but she couldn't give up the chance to be with him. To know him intimately. She caressed his chest, lingering over the well-developed pectorals.

His muscle jumped under her touch. She scraped her nail down the center line of his body. Following the fine dusting of hair that narrowed and disappeared into the waistband of his pants.

"Don't go," she said softly.

Excerpt from "Adam's Mistress" by Stephanie Grace

Adam enjoyed cooking because so many people expected him not to know how to do it. Like he was nothing more than a stereotype instead of a real person. He'd been on his own for the better part of the last fifteen years and survival demanded that he at least make an effort to learn how to feed himself.

He'd employed his parents' staff for the first five years after his parents' death, but when he learned the truth of his family's secret he felt like a fraud and couldn't in good faith continue to pretend to be someone he wasn't. One of the hardest things he'd had to do was let go of the staff. But if Molly and Hubert Johnson were working for him he wasn't going to learn to stand on his own, so he'd asked them both what they wanted to do. Molly had always longed to open a small craft store in her hometown and Adam had helped her do that. Hubert had been happy to move back home with his wife and work in the shop.

Slowly Adam had started learning what he needed to do to carve a life for himself. A life that he was in control of.

Grace wasn't one of those women who made false assumptions about him. She'd taken one look at the state of the art kitchen and understood that he would know his way around a good pot roast.

"I guess you really can cook," she said, a wry grin lighting her face.

"Yes."

"Most guys consider dinner throwing something on the grill or heating up rice in the microwave."

He wanted to groan. "A man offered to cook for you and then made microwave rice?"

She laughed but the tension didn't really ease from

her face. She was still nervous and tense. Still unsure of something.

Him, he suspected. The situation that he was engineering to hopefully get her comfortable enough that she'd share the secrets hidden behind those shadowed eyes.

"No. My dad used to make rice for us for dinner whenever there was nothing else to eat."

"Where was your mom?"

She fidgeted with the stem of her wineglass and he realized he'd probed past the bounds of what was polite conversation and gone straight into that forbidden territory marked personal. A place that it was obvious she wasn't ready to go.

"This is a really nice house. I can't believe how big all the houses are in this area."

Actually, the house was rather modest for the neighborhood, only 4,000 square feet. Certainly small compared to other properties he had around the world. But he'd liked the soaring windows and the large deck outside was a terrific place to work on the laptop on nice days. Well, it would be if he were ever here long enough to enjoy it.

Since the Johnsons had gone, he had a cleaning service come in periodically to check on things and dust. He'd had them stock the kitchen before he'd arrived. He might have to have them in more often if he truly was going to stay in Plano for the next six months.

"Where do you live?" he asked, because every detail

about her life was becoming important to him. He'd certainly be happier discussing her and her life. Maybe get her to confess she'd always been attracted to him and had written a sexy little story about the two of them.

"Not so far from the school. My subdivision is a few years old. It's a good thing I moved there when it was first built. I don't think I could afford to buy there now."

"What do you like about where you live?"

She took a sip of her wine. He finished putting the tomatoes and onions on the salmon and wrapped them in foil before putting them in the oven. He checked the boiling water and dumped in the couscous and then turned back to her. She was staring at him.

"What?"

"I thought you were faking it. That you were going to pretend to know how to cook, but then when I turned my back you'd be pulling ready-made meals from the freezer."

"No matter what else you believe about me, Grace, know that I never lie."

"*Never?* What if I asked you if this suit looked nice on me?"

"I would say that the color is good with your skin tone but that the cut isn't flattering."

She arched one eyebrow at him. "What if you get pulled over for a speeding ticket?"

"Not even then. I just don't see the point in making up a story."

"Even when you're starting a relationship? When you want to make a good impression?"

He shook his head. "That would set a tone for the relationship that I think I can fool the other person and I don't like it."

"Did someone lie to you?"

Deep inside the icy part of his soul where he hid the truth of what he was, he cringed. Lies were the very foundation his life had been built on and he hadn't even realized that until he was twenty-five. At that age when most people were coming to terms with their past, he'd learned his was a sham. "That's in the same closet that you closed the door on."

"What closet? When did I close that door?"

"The one marked personal. You closed it when you changed the subject from your mother."

"Oh. If I tell you about her…"

"I'm not trying to make a deal with you. Just saying some areas aren't meant to be trod this early in a relationship."

There were some places he didn't ever want to go. Digging into her secrets and finding out more about Grace was his only goal. He didn't want her to see him in a different light.

"Are we going to have a relationship?"

"I didn't invite the rest of the board back to my house for dinner."

"No, you didn't." She set her wineglass on the counter and walked around the island so that she stood right next to him. "Why is that? Why are you suddenly noticing me as a woman and not just as a coworker?"

He realized that he'd boxed himself into a corner. "I saw a different side of you today. I was—I am— intrigued." That was the truth.

"Desperate and willing to do anything to save the school—no wonder you're interested in me."

He laughed because he could tell she wanted to lighten the moment, but inside he knew that he shouldn't seduce her until she revealed the truth. Until she acknowledged that she'd been attracted to him for a long time.

"I don't see you as desperate."

"Well, I was. And you are turning out to be a very nice person to have in my corner."

Thinking of why he'd invited her over, he knew he wasn't nice. "No one would ever call me nice."

"I would, Adam. I know you don't see it that way, but taking a chance on me and the school…it was a very kind thing you did. And I really appreciate it."

"I don't want your appreciation."

"No?"

He shook his head, closing the distance between them and drawing her into his arms. He lowered his head, brushing his lips over hers. He told himself that he was just telling her the truth with his body because he still couldn't reveal it with his words, but he knew that something else was going on here. For the first time since he was twenty-five, he wanted to pull a woman into his arms and keep her there forever.

For a man who liked living a solitary life, that was a scary thought.

* * *

Grace rose on her tiptoes to meet Adam's mouth. She snaked her arms around his waist and held on to him, afraid to wake from the dream that he'd enveloped her in. For some reason, Adam Bowen was suddenly paying attention to her and she didn't want to let him go.

The worries she'd carried for the last ten days faded to the back of her mind. He opened his mouth and she knew he'd said something but for the life of her she couldn't hear him over the roaring in her ears. She kept her eyes open as he moved closer to her.

"Grace?"

"Hmm?"

"Last chance…"

She realized he was telling her to pull back but she couldn't. He was her fantasy and after the long stressful day she'd had, she wanted—no, needed—to put her needs first. She'd wanted to kiss Adam since the first moment they'd met.

His lips brushed over hers. *Adam Bowen was kissing her.* He tasted way better than she'd imagined he would. He kept his touch light, his tongue tracing the seam between her lips. She let her eyes drift closed and knew that she'd made a choice that was going to change the nice safe world she'd created for herself.

The timer on the oven beeped and he pulled back. Reluctantly. He directed her toward the dining room and she went in by herself, knowing she needed to collect her thoughts and find her center.

What if he was toying with her? One other time, she'd believed in a man and he'd disappointed her badly. She didn't want to be a fool again, but Adam had always seemed different to her.

The dining room was ultra-formal, decorated in dark wood and antiques. This was the kind of showplace house her father would have eyed with a fanatical gleam, sure the owner had plenty of spare cash to donate to the church. The kind of place she'd never have been invited into as a child.

She heard Adam's footsteps behind her and turned as he entered the room. He set the plates on the table and held out a chair for her. Once seated she muttered a quick prayer of thanks under her breath.

Then glanced up in time to see him take his seat. The meal was delicious and she wanted to keep the conversation light. To remind herself that no matter what Adam intimated, this wasn't the beginning of a personal relationship.

But she wanted to know more about him. She wanted to find out why he had a thing about lying. Most people paid lip service to believing in that, but in real life often rattled off falsehoods without a second thought.

She should just ask him straight out if he'd seen the story in her office and maybe picked it up. But she'd be so embarrassed if she had to explain about it. What if it wasn't Adam? Jose, Bruce and other staffers went in and out of her office all the time. Even students and other teachers had access.

For just one night, she wanted to see the real man so that when she got home after this strange day was over, she could write down her impressions of him. The way his hand had felt on hers. The way his lips had moved over hers. The way he'd cocked his head to the side and really listened while she talked about subjects on which no one else wanted her opinion.

Even if she never saw him again, she knew he'd given her a gift. But she *would* see him again. And she didn't want to slip back into invisible mode with him. The weight of her hair against her shoulders reminded her that he already saw her in a different light.

"What were your parents like?" she asked, when they'd finished their main course and were having coffee on his deck. It overlooked the well-landscaped backyard. In the center of the yard was a large pool with a waterfall on the far end.

"Ward and June Cleaver. Are you old enough to know who they are?" he asked.

"I think everyone has seen *Leave It to Beaver* on Nick@Nite."

"Very funny. My mom and dad were the perfect parents, doting, supportive, strict when they needed to be."

"So why haven't you settled down?" she asked. It was the one thing she'd always wondered about him. He seemed so perfect—what was stopping him from committing to one of the perfect women he dated?

"Why haven't you?" he asked.

She swallowed hard. This was why she didn't do

close relationships. Sooner or later you had to talk about your past. Small talk only lasted so long. "I didn't grow up with the perfect parents."

"What kind of childhood did you have?" he asked.

It was an innocent question. She wanted to counter with a change of topic—something to turn the spotlight back on him—but she wasn't going to, because she did want to get to know Adam better. And that thing he'd said earlier about trust had struck a nerve. Here was a man she thought she could trust.

"I don't know. One like most kids. I think you're the exception, Adam." In her small town, he would have been the exception. They'd had rich kids like everywhere else, but no one who'd grown up the way Adam had. Traveling every season, going to trendy ski resorts and all-inclusive Caribbean getaways instead of riding in the backseat of a cramped car to some dreary relative's house several hours away.

"How?" he asked, his interest genuine.

"Just that a lot of parents weren't that supportive of kids in my neighborhood."

"You're from a small town, right?"

"Yes. A poor one. Most families really scrambled to make a living."

"Yours?"

"Yes."

"What did your folks do?"

She should never have started this conversation. How could she talk about being deprived when her father had been a preacher and had provided a nice house for her? How could she explain, without sounding like a whiner, exactly the way she'd been deprived? How could she explain what she herself never wanted to understand?

"My dad's a preacher."

"So you're the rebellious preacher's daughter?"

"No. Not a rebel. I prefer to just blend into the walls."

"I've noticed."

"Well I must be doing something wrong, because you weren't supposed to notice."

"I didn't until today."

She smiled at the way he said it. Like it was an important thing. That having noticed her had made a difference to him.

Was it because of the story?

"I've noticed you before."

"Really? Tell me what you observed."

She took her time trying to figure out how to tell him what she'd seen in him without revealing how deeply she'd studied him. Now that she was here with him, she felt a little silly that she'd given him a starring role in her fantasies without really knowing the man behind the good looks.

Adam knew he was pushing. But the more he learned about Grace, the more he realized that his knowing about her fantasies was going to wound her. She gave off the image of being so superefficient and competent that only tonight had he glimpsed the vulnerabilities she had underneath.

He didn't want her to think he'd exploited those weaknesses. And guilt ate at him. Omissions were lies, he thought. Hell, he knew that omissions were the biggest kind of lies.

But he wanted to hear from her lips that she found him attractive. That he hadn't imagined the story that he'd reread during the day about five times. He knew exactly what she liked. How she wanted a man who was forceful in the bedroom but sensitive and understanding outside.

To be honest, that wasn't how he normally operated with a woman, but everything about Grace was different. She made him want to be more. He didn't know why. He couldn't explain it to himself. But tonight, with a cool breeze in the air and the fragrance of the blooming vegetation around his pool filling the air, he didn't care.

He didn't want to think of anything other than this woman and how he could convince her she'd be safe in his arms. And he wanted her in his arms. He wanted her mouth under his with no dinner buzzer about to go off. No crowded restaurant of people too close to them. Just the two of them and the night and nothing between them.

"Come on, Grace, what did you think about me the first time we met?" he asked, having the feeling that she was going to just keep quiet and let the conversation die an awkward death.

"It's complicated," she said, leaving the deck and

walking toward the pool. She stopped by a potted hibiscus and bent to smell the bloom.

She ran whenever he pushed too far into her barriers. The ones she used to keep everyone at arm's length. She was subtle and only someone who spent a significant amount of time with her as he had today would notice it.

"I understand complicated. Is it such a bad impression that you're worried about hurting my feelings?"

"Give me a break. You must know that no one has a bad first impression of you."

"I don't know that, Gracie. You won't tell me what you thought."

She took a deep breath and faced him, her eyes alive with an emotion he couldn't name. "I thought, this man is someone who knows how to really live his life."

He was taken aback by her comment. To be honest, he'd been fishing for a compliment. Having read her story, he knew she liked his shoulders and his backside. He was chagrined to realize that he'd expected her impressions to just be physical. If they had been, he would have felt comfortable using the physical attraction between the two of them to seduce her.

"Not what you were expecting?" she asked.

"No," he said. What she'd observed in him revealed what she herself was afraid she was missing. It took him a moment to identify fragility and fear as the emotions in her eyes. Grace didn't lie, either. The knowledge made him feel protective of her.

"Well, there it is. You also have very nice eyes."

She took a step closer to him. There were still a few

inches of space between them, but she'd made a move toward him—the first she'd made since they met. He was a little thrown by her compliment. Nice eyes? "No one has ever mentioned that before."

She wiggled her eyebrows at him. "Probably because they were busy ogling your physique."

"Ah, that's more what I was expecting."

She laughed at him. But there was something in her eyes that told him she'd said it to distract him. And he let her because he already knew more of her secrets than he intended. More than she'd probably intended him to know.

"Anything specific about my physique?" he asked, letting her turn this moment a little lighter. He had to touch her again. She'd left her hair down. The silky length of it fell around her shoulders, curling gently.

He caught one of the curls and let it wrap around his hand and wrist, drawing her closer to him. She was short, shorter than he'd realized until he held her in his arms. She came only to his shoulders.

He lowered his head, brushing his lips against hers. He felt her fingers move restlessly on him and wished he didn't have his shirt on so he could feel her touch on his skin.

Her fingers were small and her touch light. So light and tentative, as if she wasn't sure what to do next. He groaned deep in his chest, thinking of this fragile, beautiful woman and wondering if he had a right to touch her like this. Because he was a rambler. A rolling stone that had learned that life was less painful when he kept moving. He didn't notice the emptiness when he moved from place to place.

And if ever a woman was rooted to one place, it was Grace.

She opened her lips under his and he stopped thinking. He just felt. The soft brush of her tongue over the seam of his lips made his blood flow heavy. He felt a tingle of arousal spread down his spine. He pulled her closer with his hand in her hair at the back of her neck.

His other hand skimmed down her curves to rest on her hip, drawing her into his body before he took control of the kiss, thrusting his tongue deep into her mouth and tasting her deeply. The flavor of the wine they'd had with dinner was on her tongue, but also something he was beginning to identify with only Grace. That was what he hungered for. More Grace.

He lifted her to his body, canted his hips and wrapped his arm strongly around her hips to enable him to kiss her deeper. To thrust his tongue into her mouth again and again, trying to assuage a hunger that he'd never had before. A hunger that made all the emptiness in his life pale in comparison. A hunger that came from this small, complicated woman.

Five

He traced her lips, his finger following the path
his mouth had taken a few moments earlier. He
caressed the pulse point where he'd suckled her
neck and then moved lower.

His stomach was rock hard and rippled when he
moved. He reached around her back and
unhooked her bra and then pushed the cups up out
of his way. He pulled her closer until the tips of
her breasts brushed his chest.

"Grace." He said her name like a promise.

Excerpt from "Adam's Mistress" by Stephanie Grace

He overwhelmed her. Adam had literally swept Grace
off her feet and she didn't care. For once it felt good to

just forget about everything and feel. She wrapped her arms around his shoulders and gave herself up to his embrace.

She shifted restlessly in his arms, trying to get closer to him. She felt the world spinning around her and found and felt the padded cushion of a lounge chair under her back. Adam pulled back for a second, shifting her to her side and sliding down on the chair next to her. He pulled her back into his arms.

Actually being in his embrace, feeling the length of his body pressed against hers was so much better than she'd imagined. He was dominant and a little aggressive but she felt cherished in his arms. She knew he'd never hurt her. She was startled by that thought. It had been years since she'd thought of a man's strength being used against her.

He traced his hand over her face as if he were memorizing her features. There was so much heat in his eyes, she was surprised she could still breathe. She wanted to feed that fire and make him forget the outer trappings of the plain woman she'd worked so hard to project. But she wanted to be equal to him in this moment. She wanted to be alive instead of just blending into the background.

She tunneled her fingers through his hair, holding his head still. He waited for her to make her next move. She shifted in his arms so that her head was above his, her elbows resting on his chest, and she lowered her mouth to his. Rubbed her lips over his. Because she wanted to make this moment last forever.

She wanted to remember every millisecond of this

kiss and how he tasted and felt. His lips were firm and strong and she just breathed into his mouth for a second before sliding her tongue beyond his teeth deep into his mouth.

He groaned and tightened his hand on the back of her head, rolling her to her side again so that she was cradled in the crook of his arm as he took complete control of the kiss. His other hand rubbed her back, then slowly slipped around to the front of her body. He rested his hand on her abdomen and she tensed, knowing she wasn't model slim or perfect, but he soothed her with long, drugging kisses that proved he was attracted to her.

Really attracted. She couldn't think as he unbuttoned her blouse. He pulled back from her mouth, trailing kisses down her jaw to her neck. He buried his face against her and inhaled deeply and she held him to her. As he nibbled on her skin, his tongue found the pulse beating strongly at the base of her neck and suckled it.

Shivers coursed down her arms and torso. Her breasts felt full and achy and she arched in his arms, trying to rub them against his chest. But there was just enough distance between their bodies that she couldn't.

He put his hand between her breasts. His palm, hot against her skin where the edges of her blouse parted, made her nipples tighten and she tried to rotate her shoulders to bring them in contact with his hand. But he held her still underneath him.

He pushed the sleeves of her blouse down her arms.

She sat up to let him remove it. She reached for the buttons on his shirt, wanting to keep things equal between them because she knew she was already out of control.

He urged her back again, with his hand between her breasts, and leaned up over her, his hand moving over her torso. Her breasts were covered by the lacy cups of her bra and her stomach was only partially visible, her suit skirt covering her belly button. She was wearing control-top panty hose, she thought, but then he brought a finger to her face.

Tracing a path down her nose to her mouth, he outlined her lips and then moved lower, his finger following the path his mouth had taken a few minutes earlier. He caressed the pulse point where he'd suckled her neck and then feathered over the fabric of her bra, tracing the edges until she was shifting underneath him, trying to get him to touch her without having to ask.

He slid his finger under the fabric of her bra and caressed the globe of her breast briefly before withdrawing and tracing the line between her breasts down to the waistband of her skirt.

He did this over and over again until she was out of her mind with needing him.

She grabbed his hand and placed it over her breast. Held his palm over her lace-covered nipple and rubbed herself against him. She closed her eyes and shifted under him. Needing more.

He tugged his hand out from under hers and lowered his head. His warm breath brushed over her distended nipple first, then his lips rubbed back and forth over her before she felt the delicate bite of his teeth.

She moaned, wanting so much more. There was an ache deep inside her that she thought would never be alleviated. He started suckling her breast. Her legs moved restlessly and she tried to draw him over her. She wanted his weight on her. She wanted something solid to hold on to while his mouth drove her further down the path of arousal.

She felt his hand on her thigh, moving up a panty-hose-clad leg and under her skirt. He continued to suckle her as his fingers teased her inner thighs, moving closer and closer to the warm center of her body. To the place where she wanted to feel his fingers so badly. But he held her in his embrace, building her passion to the breaking point but not letting her go over.

He moved to her other breast and the cool evening air on her wet, tight nipple made her groan again. She moved her hands restlessly up and down his back and finally she felt his hand slip under the waistband of her panty hose.

He rested his hand on her lower stomach, lifted his head and glanced down at her. Waiting for permission to touch her so intimately. She knew she'd die if he didn't but she had no words to say what she wanted.

"Please, Adam."

He smiled at her, lowering his head to take her mouth again in a passionate kiss while his fingers moved through the damp curls between her legs.

* * *

Adam hadn't meant the evening to go as far as it had, but there was something so addictive about the feel and taste of Grace that he couldn't stop. He didn't want to stop until he was buried hilt deep in her silky body.

She responded so beautifully to him. He wanted to surround himself completely in her. She was damp and ready for him. He pushed his forefinger through her damp curls, touching her intimately. She clutched at his shoulders, holding him tightly as if to keep him from leaving her. As if he'd leave at this moment. He needed her response. It made him feel alive in a way he didn't want to examine too closely.

He bent to her breast again, drawing her turgid nipple into his mouth. Sucking on her strongly, trying to draw some essence of Grace into his own body. She lifted herself up into his embrace, her legs falling open to give his hand more room to move between them.

He lifted his head from her breast, pushing her skirt to her waist and drawing her panty hose and underwear down her body and off. Her legs were firm and soft and her body much slimmer than the boxy clothing she wore revealed. She had lush hips that he sank his fingers into. Once he had bared her to his gaze, he pushed her legs apart. She shifted on the lounge chair, moving restlessly.

He parted her with his fingers, lowering his head, needing to know if she tasted as good here as her mouth and breasts had. He tongued her gently and parted her with his thumbs. She cried out, her hips rising to meet his mouth. Her hands moved restlessly from his head to his shoulders, her thighs clenching around him and then falling apart.

He sensed it wouldn't take much to drive her over the edge. Licking delicately at her, he lifted her hips in his hands, his fingers sinking into her buttocks and cradling her so that he held her completely open to him.

"Adam…"

"Hmm?"

"I'm not going to last much longer."

"Good," he said. He draped her thighs over his shoulders and gave himself up to making Grace lose control, to seeing the flush of her skin deepen and listen to the breathy moans that were the sweetest music he'd heard in a long time.

He used his fingers to tease her until she was arching into his touch, and then he bit carefully on her most delicate flesh, sucking her into his mouth while he pushed one finger deep inside her.

Her body clenched around his fingers, heels digging into his back as she moved frantically.

His name was a long sigh on her lips as her climax rushed through her body. He kept his mouth and fingers on her until the internal clenching of her body stopped and then he moved up her body, keeping his hand between her legs as he found her breasts once again, suckling on them, hoping to find some satisfaction from just touching her.

She reached between their bodies, found him painfully engorged. She scraped her fingernail down the side of his zipper. He tightened even more.

Slowly she pulled the tab of his zipper, reaching into his pants and through the opening in his boxers to touch his hot flesh.

She circled him with her hand, stroking up and down and he lifted his head from her breast, brought his mouth down on hers, letting her taste herself.

She pulled her mouth from his. "Open your legs, Adam."

He shifted them apart and felt her hand move lower, cupping him and rolling her fingers over him. He tightened.

"Grace, you need to stop."

"Why?"

He explained why in blunt detail.

"Yes," she said.

"Yes?"

"I want that," she said.

He growled her name and bent to take her mouth again. Her hand worked up and down his length until he knew he wouldn't be able to hold back any longer.

He shifted his hips, wanting to move away from her, but she tightened her grip, driving him over the edge. She tangled her other hand in the hair at the back of his neck and drew his mouth down to hers.

He lowered his head to her breast, resting there. Feeling the emptiness that was always inside him ebb for the first time in a long time.

She wrapped her arms around his shoulders and one

of her legs over his hips. And held him, and he let her. Not wanting to acknowledge that he had found a weakness in himself that only this woman had brought out.

Adam lifted her into his arms and carried her into the dark house. She wrapped her arms around his shoulders, not really wanting to talk. She was afraid that if she did this moment would drift away and she'd wake up. Realize this was a beautiful fantasy instead of reality.

She caught a glimpse of his bedroom—king-size bed dominating one side of the room, floor-to-ceiling windows with crisp sheers pulled across them—as he walked into the master bath and set her on her feet. He turned on the lighting over the garden tub and the largest shower she'd ever seen. It was a glass enclosed structure with two showerheads on opposite ends.

She was aware of her state of disarray. A twinge of embarrassment went through her. But then she glanced at Adam, who was equally disheveled.

He caught her glance and drew her closer to him, kissing her once again. She wanted more. She wanted to feel him hot and hard between her legs. She wanted him to lose control again only this time inside her so that she'd carry his mark on her and in her.

He drew back. "I'll put some clean clothes on the counter."

She watched him walk away and felt a little colder. She didn't do sex well. She always associated it with some kind of deeper feelings, and maybe Adam didn't.

Of course he didn't. He'd said at dinner that he'd never noticed her until today. She wrapped her arms around her waist, feeling small and oh, she didn't like this feeling.

She removed her clothing quickly and turned on the shower, wanting—no, needing—to get clean and get out of here. What the hell had she been thinking? She had to *work* with Adam. He was staying in town to help her and she was going to have to sit across from him in meetings and remember the way his mouth had felt on her breasts. The way he had felt in her hand.

She stepped into the shower and lifted her head toward the water, hoping it would wash away the feelings that were overwhelming her. She braced one arm on the wall and tried to find her center.

But her center had always come from that core deep inside her that no one had ever realized was there. And tonight she'd let Adam see it. She knew it was going to be impossible to pretend this hadn't happened.

The shower door opened and Adam stepped into the cubicle. She glanced up at him, praying that what she felt wasn't on her face.

He didn't say anything, just drew her into his arms, holding her naked body against his. She closed her eyes and rested her head on his chest. His scent surrounded her and diminished the panic that had been growing steadily since he'd brought her into the bathroom.

"What's wrong?" he asked.

His deep voice brushed over her, sounding like

something straight out of her dreams. Tears burned the back of her eyes, because she had dreamed so many times of him holding her like this.

"I'm not…oh, heck, Adam. I'm not used to getting so intimate so fast."

He rubbed his hand up and down her back. "Don't think about that. Whatever's between us is different."

For her, she knew that. But she was positive that Adam was used to women falling all over him and she wanted to be distinctive, not part of the pack.

He tipped her head back. "What are you thinking?"

"That I'm an idiot."

"Gracie…"

"No one's ever called me a nickname before," she said, the words slipping out without her permission.

She'd had two serious relationships since she'd left home and neither of them had lasted more than a year. She was afraid suddenly that Adam would be gone as quickly. Not because she needed a man to cling to, but because he was the first person to make her feel like who she was was enough. That she didn't have to pretend to be someone else. And that really scared her, because she'd never been comfortable in her own skin.

"Can I ask you a personal question?" he asked.

"I'm standing naked in your shower. I think we've gone past the point where personal questions are out of bounds."

"Why do you wear baggy clothes?"

"I… They're just more comfortable."

"I thought we agreed there'd be no lies between us."

"Did we agree to that?"

"Stop stalling."

She reached for the loofah sponge and put some shower gel on it. "Turn around and I'll wash your back."

He arched one eyebrow at her but did as she asked. She scrubbed his back and noticed the scar that ran along the base of his spine. She touched it, wondering where it came from. "I wear the baggy clothes because my body distracts men. Makes them think of sin instead of business."

"Grace."

She stepped away from him, retreating to the far corner of the shower, sponging herself. Actually, now that she'd said the words out loud, she knew that she'd revealed too much. She felt more naked than she had on the lounge chair with his mouth between her legs.

"I don't know who said that to you, but that is not what your body makes me think of."

She tipped her head to the side, studying him. Trying to gauge the truth in his words. "What do I make you think of, Adam?"

He dropped his gaze from her for a second and then lifted his eyes to hers again. "You make me think of home, Gracie."

She didn't know how to respond to that, and it seemed neither did Adam. They each washed their own hair and got out of the shower without saying another word. It scared her to realize that Adam knew some of her deepest secrets, but she knew she also knew one of his. The man who had everything his heart desired was searching for something the same way she was.

Six

The sound of raised voices filtered through her locked office door. Panicked at the thought of getting caught half naked in his arms, she started to push away from him.

But he held her close, wrapping his strong arms around her. "I've got you."

Grace hugged him to her and closed her eyes, reminding herself that this was just loneliness and she hadn't found the man she'd been secretly dreaming of.

Excerpt from "Adam's Mistress" by Stephanie Grace

Two weeks later, Grace had managed to keep Adam at arm's length. Not an easy decision on her part, but she knew that dating him publicly was the absolute worst thing she could do as an administrator. Plus, she was scared.

She would admit it only to herself, but she'd let Adam get much closer in one night that she'd ever intended to. Seeing him every day at the school was a bittersweet thing. After hearing from two concerned parents about the amount of time she was spending with Adam on campus, she was almost afraid to be alone with him.

Afraid that if anyone thought there was something inappropriate going on between her and Adam, it might fuel Malcolm's campaign to close the school. Sue-Ellen and the PTA had really run with the fundraising and money was starting to come in from the alumni group. But Grace knew any small mistake could set Malcolm off.

More disconcerting, her file folder with the story had shown back up on her desk. Where had it been? Had it been there the entire time?

She glanced at the pages and knew she should probably shred the thing before someone definitely saw it. The office shredder was in Bruce's cubicle and she'd tried a couple of times to use it but someone always walked by.

There was a brief knock on her door before it opened and Adam filled the doorway.

She shoved the folder under the blotter on her desk. She flushed a little and hated that. She wanted to come off as more sophisticated than she was, but no matter how hard she tried she was always going to be a small-town girl.

"Good afternoon, Grace. Do you have a minute?" Adam asked.

Quickly she closed the Internet window on her computer where she'd been reading an article about Adam that had been in *Entrepreneur* magazine last fall.

"Sure," she said.

He closed the door behind him. He wore a pair of dark dress pants and a blue shirt that really brought out his eyes.

"Please leave the door open."

"What?"

"Sue-Ellen thinks I'm spending too much time with you behind closed doors. You know she goes straight to Malcolm with her concerns, so I really don't want to give her any more fodder."

He crossed his arms over his chest and made no move to open the door. She didn't want to force the issue. Worrying about a closed door seemed kind of silly to her, but she was willing to do whatever was needed to keep the school open.

"Is that why you've been too busy to have dinner with me the last two weeks?" he asked.

"No. I have a life. I wasn't just sitting alone in my house waiting for you to start asking me out." She hoped he'd never know how many nights she'd spent sitting alone in her house thinking of him. Fantasizing about what it would be like to be in his arms. Her dreams had now become fevered remembrances of his mouth on her body. Her hands on him. She squirmed a little in her chair just at the thought of the intimacies they'd shared.

"Too bad for me," he said with a self-deprecating grin that made her smile back at him.

"What did you want to discuss?" she asked, knowing if she didn't change the subject she was going to do something she'd regret, like tell him to lock the door then seduce him on her desk.

"The gym needs a new floor. And that's not in your budget," he said, leaning back against the still-closed door.

"What do you suggest we do?" she asked. The school needed a lot of repairs. The tuitions that they'd had to refund after the scandal broke had left them in a sticky place.

"Coach Jarrett and the boys' team suggested a charity basketball game to raise money. We'd use the outdoor courts for play."

That was a great idea, but she wondered how many games they'd have to play to earn enough money to re-surface the floor. "Okay. But I don't think we're going to raise enough with just our team. Attendance at the games hasn't been that high."

"I'm going to contact a few of the musicians on my label and get them to come and play."

"I approve that idea. When were you thinking of having the event?"

"The weekend prior to spring break. I think that will give us some high-profile press coverage and we can maximize it to bring our enrollment numbers up."

"Sounds good. I have some local media contacts we can use. And Barbara Langdon would be a great parent to coordinate this. She's super-organized. Do you want me to set that up?"

"Yes. I've given Bruce all the information on the artists I think will participate."

She made a few notes on her computer calendar. Adam came farther into her office, leaning one hip on the side of her desk right next to her.

"Now that we've got school business out of the way…."

She pushed her chair away from the desk to put more space between them. "Yes?"

"I've got tickets to the Stars. Want to join me?" he asked.

She wanted to say yes. She'd never been to a professional sports game. Ever. And the Dallas Stars were a really good hockey team. She knew they were going for the Stanley Cup.

But more than any interest in sports, she wanted to spend time with Adam. To feed the obsession that had grown in the weeks when they'd been dealing with each other only for the school's business. "I'm not sure that's a good idea. What will the board think?"

"I don't care."

"That's easy for you to say. If the school closes down, you still have a job."

"Do you think I'm that callous?"

"No," she said. "But I do think you're used to everyone doing what you want them to."

"What are you afraid of?"

"Why do I have to be afraid? Malcolm is just looking for an excuse to get the board to fire me."

"Going to a hockey game with me isn't going to affect your job."

He had a point. She knew it. But she was starting to care for him and she was afraid if they got any closer that she was never going to recover when he moved on. And he would move on, because there wasn't anything to hold him here in Plano. She wasn't the kind of woman that made a man stop roaming around. Much as she wanted to be.

"Okay," she said, realizing that she was running from herself again. She had to stop running away if she really wanted to find herself.

Adam was surprised by how challenging he found the work at Tremmel-Bowen. The school was one of those connections to his parents that he'd distanced himself from. They'd been very involved in the running of the school and, at twenty-five, when he'd learned the truth about himself, he'd been angry. Carrying on his family's traditions hadn't seemed important.

But without intending to, Grace was giving him a chance to see the pride that his father must have felt in the school. Talking to the students and seeing the campus, he felt a connection to the Bowens that he'd lost when he'd heard a few sentences uttered from a distant relative. A relative who had made the loving family he'd always taken for granted a big lie.

It was why he was a stickler about the truth.

Tonight he promised himself that he would bring up the subject of Grace's erotic story. He'd find a way to make her tell him about it and then admit he'd read it.

He knew they'd both retreated after the intimacy they'd shared on his pool deck. And he'd come to some strange conclusions about himself and Grace. No matter why he'd first become attracted to her, the need to know her and bind her to him had grown.

He rang the doorbell at her house a few minutes early. Grace lived in a neatly kept townhome community. A small, wrought-iron bench sat to the left on her small porch and a Welcome wreath hung on the door. The scene felt welcoming in a way he associated only with Grace.

He heard her footsteps on some kind of hardwood or tile floor before the door opened. She had her hair pulled back in a ponytail and wore a pair of baggy jeans and a cute pink T-shirt. He smiled to himself at the way she carefully concealed her curvy body.

He didn't like that she hid that part of herself. She had the kind of body that he'd always dreamed of holding. And she was embarrassed by it. Her words—that she was made for sin—still lingered in the back of his mind.

Even if he left Grace with nothing other than the school, he'd first make her see herself through his eyes. To see that she was so much more than that long-ago image she had of herself.

"I just need to put on my shoes and change my purse. Do you want to come in for a drink?"

"That would be nice," he said, catching a glimpse of

her decor over her shoulder. The floor was a dark hardwood, probably oak. A coat tree stood to one side, hung with Grace's coats, and a brightly colored scarf lay draped over a small table.

She led the way through her house. It was elegantly decorated with some homey touches—photos on the mantel, antiques in the hallways. As he glanced around her private sanctuary he realized he was seeing another layer of that private woman. The house suited her.

"I've got iced tea, beer and some white wine," she said, opening the refrigerator and glancing inside it.

"Tea would be great."

"It's not sweet."

"Perfect." He realized she was nervous about having him here. And he liked that. She was always so confident of herself, moving through life as though nothing really bothered her, that he liked shaking her up.

She got a glass with ice and poured the tea. She set it on the breakfast bar and moved to the other side of the kitchen, leaning against the counter next to the refrigerator and watching him as if she wasn't sure what to do with him.

"I'm not going to pounce on you now that we're finally alone again." Though he wanted to. His arms were empty without her in them. He wanted to kiss and caress her, to keep their relationship on a level that he easily understood, and fit the mold of what he expected from the women in his life, instead of dealing with all the other things that she brought to the surface. The longings for home and permanency that he'd thought he'd shed a long time ago.

"I didn't think you would," she said with a tart note in her voice.

"Then what's up?" he asked, after taking a sip of his iced tea.

She shrugged. "My house is so much smaller than yours."

He was coming to realize that one of Grace's major hang-ups was the fact that she was conscious of what other people had and measured herself against them. Why would she think he'd be judging her by the size of her house?

If she knew the truth about him—the fact that he was a fake Bowen—she might not care that his house was bigger than hers. But he knew it was *his* money, the money he'd earned on his own, that provided the basis for his wealth. He'd taken his parents' entire fortune and donated it to charities that he knew his mother would have supported.

"I like your house, Gracie. It's a lot like you."

"How?" she asked, wrapping her arms around her waist. He had the feeling that if he said the wrong thing she was going to retreat even further into herself and disappear completely.

"Well, this kitchen is bright and welcoming. Your house if filled with photos and antiques, stuff that has a lasting feeling to it."

She nodded and her arms dropped to her sides. "I always wanted roots. When I was growing up, my father served in a lot of different communities in Texas. We were constantly moving."

"And you've put them down." He knew she had. The way she spoke about moving made it very clear exactly what she thought of it. He realized that, if there was going to be any real lasting relationship between the two of them, he'd have to change his ways. And he wondered if she would be worth staying for.

She nodded. "The antiques aren't heirlooms. I bought them at auctions and estate sales."

"That doesn't change what they represent about you."

She bit her lower lip. "I'll be quick getting ready."

"Take your time. Do you mind if I explore your house?"

She released a long breath. "Okay."

Grace enjoyed having Adam in her house. He was the missing piece of the puzzle that she'd created of a picture-perfect life. He'd been the fantasy in her head for a long time, the man who'd make this little empty house feel more like home—and now he was here.

Her fear was that she only liked him because he did fill the hole in her life. That she wasn't infatuated with a real man. It was complicated and she wanted it to be simple. For a relationship with Adam to be easier than it was.

She'd wasted some time when she'd gotten home, writing down her latest fantasy about him. In her dream relationship, he was completely enthralled with her and her body.

She finished getting ready and then went to find Adam. To her dismay, he was in her home office, sitting at her desk. She knew that her handwritten notes on "Adam's Mistress" were there. The printed copy of her story was still at work, but she'd been editing a handwritten version of it earlier that day, adding in details from the night at his home.

She noticed he was studying something on her desk. For a second, she couldn't breathe. She'd die if he'd found that story. In fact, tomorrow she was going to shred the thing at work and destroy this copy.

"You like Viper?" he asked.

For a minute it was as if he were speaking a different language. Then she realized her mouse pad featured the heavy metal alternative band.

"Yes. I do. Their music is different."

"You know they're one of my artists. Actually, the first band I signed."

"I did know that," she said. She'd checked them out originally because she knew that Adam liked them.

"I can get you an autograph," he said, with one of those silly grins of his.

"Really. Then maybe I'll like you."

He laughed, a full-bodied one that made her feel good. "All the girls say that, but as soon as they get their autograph…"

"I'm not like other girls, Adam."

He pushed to his feet and came around the front of her desk. It was a cheap one that she'd gotten at a scratch-and-dent sale. He leaned against the front of it, legs crossed at the ankles, arms resting on either side of his hips.

"I know that."

"Why are you here? I mean really. I'm not your usual type of date."

She'd tried not to think about him. Had focused on the school and keeping it going. But in the back of her mind she'd been looking for excuses to keep him at arm's length. Not because she didn't want him closer but because she feared what would happen if she did and it turned out he wasn't as interested in her.

"I think we've discussed this before."

She envied him his ease and self-confidence in this situation. She'd handled herself with aplomb when she'd had to confront two teachers having sex in a classroom but this was simply beyond the scope of her experience. Adam was beyond that scope, and she hoped he'd never realize by how much.

"I think you're right, but I still don't get it. It seems like this is some sort of dream and that I'm going to wake up and you'll still be treating me like a stranger."

"Am I your dream man?" he asked.

She slid her gaze down his body. Dressed in an oxford shirt with the collar open and a pair of faded, tight jeans, he looked like every woman's dream man. But it was way more than just his sexy, muscular body that made him her fantasy.

She shrugged, afraid of saying something and revealing too much to him. Afraid of increasing the very real chance that he might see her as a pathetic woman who'd somehow gotten hold of him and wouldn't let go. Afraid that he'd realize she wasn't the kind of woman who could hold his attention.

"Am I, Grace?" he asked, pushing away from the desk and walking toward her.

"Yes."

"For how long?" he asked.

"Why? Why does that matter?"

"Because I want to know every one of your secrets," he said, stopping with just an inch of space between them.

He was in her personal space but she didn't care. She wanted him closer. It had been two long weeks since she'd felt his arms around her, and it had been too easy to convince herself that she'd simply dreamed the way he'd felt in her arms.

"My secrets?" He could never know her secrets. She didn't like the fact that he'd even guessed that there was more to her than what she presented to the people she worked with.

But at the same time, that was what drew her even closer to him. She liked that he was the only man who saw beyond her facade. And if there was some safe way to let him in and still protect her tender heart, she'd do it.

"Yes, Gracie, your secrets," he said. He cupped her jaw and tipped her head back, his fingers supporting the back of her neck as he kissed her.

"Do you have secrets, Adam?" she whispered.

"We all do."

She clenched her hands together and stood still in his

embrace. She didn't know if she trusted him enough. If she'd ever trust him enough—because even after spending time in his arms, she still didn't think he was real. He was still just a fantasy, and if they were ever going to get to a point of trust she was going to have to let him be real.

And the real man was complicated. He had problems and issues just like she did. He moved on. He always moved on. What kind of secrets did he have that he was always searching for something but never finding it?

She realized in that instant with his mouth on hers and his hand on her neck that she wanted to be the keeper of his secrets. That she wanted to find a way to understand the complex man who had been her fantasy for too long and that she now wanted to be her reality.

But he couldn't be as long as their relationship remained hidden. She knew what happened to secrets like this. Forbidden desires were forbidden for a reason. A relationship that started in lies would never survive.

She had the uneasy feeling that she was going to be forced to choose between the safe place she'd made for herself at Tremmel-Bowen and Adam. The tightening in her gut told her the day was closer than she wanted it to be.

Seven

"I don't know why we have to hide from the world," he said.

He wouldn't understand. But she wasn't one of the glamorous women he was always seen with. Everyone would take one look at them and know she wasn't meant to be on his arm.

"Please, Adam. I don't want to share what we have found together. They'll think I'm your mistress." And she was, wasn't she?

"Okay, Grace. For you."

The voices moved on down the hallway and he stared down at her. She knew that something had changed between them in those few moments.

Excerpt from "Adam's Mistress" by Stephanie Grace

Adam had never enjoyed a hockey game more. Though Grace knew little about the sport, she learned quickly. Normally he would have been annoyed but wasn't surprised to find that with Grace he wasn't.

They were sitting alone in the luxury box that Adam shared. The box had a wet bar staffed by an arena worker plus two TV monitors so they wouldn't miss any of the action they might not catch from the bird's-eye view through the huge bay window that overlooked the arena. Adam had asked that one TV be tuned to CNN so he could keep track of Viper lead singer Stevie Taylor, who was Larry King's guest for the evening.

"I've never really gotten into professional sports," Grace said as the game reached the end of the second quarter.

"My dad was a huge hockey fan. We went to every Stars game, even the away ones."

"What was he like? I know he was big on community involvement, and the community-service program he established at Tremmel-Bowen is one of the things that really makes us stand out from other schools."

Adam noticed that Grace never forgot about the school or her commitment to it. He wished there was a way for Malcolm to see this side of Grace. So he'd understand that just because Dawn had made him look like a chump, the school didn't need to be closed down.

"He was a good man like you said, big on community involvement, but he also made sure that he had time for me. My folks were in their forties and well established before I came along."

"I didn't realize that. Were you a very spoiled only child?"

"To some extent. Not in material things." It had been a long time since he'd really thought about his parents and his childhood. He'd pushed those memories away at twenty-five and had been afraid to look back and see if he'd fooled himself into believing that the love they'd showered on him had been a lie.

"I never had a lot of material things, either," she said quietly.

"Are you an only child? I thought there were some pictures on your mantel of some other people your age. I assumed they were siblings."

She flushed and looked away, reaching over to pick up her soda cup she took a long swallow. What was she hiding about her family?

He already had the impression that she hadn't had a very nice upbringing. He sensed that the key to figuring this woman out lay in her past. After all, the things *he* was hiding all stemmed from that one incident. That one comment that had shaped his life from twenty-five forward and made him question everything that had gone on before.

"Tell me," he said, wanting her to trust him. He didn't question why gaining her trust was so important. He only knew that with Grace it was one of the things he wouldn't compromise on.

"Tell you what?"

"Whatever it is about those pictures that made you turn several interesting shades of red."

"I'm going to sound like a loser," she said.

He cupped the back of her neck and drew her toward him, leaning down to kiss her. To tell her with his embrace that he believed in her. "Never."

"I don't know what to do with you," she said. The words sounded like a confession and he knew to some extent they were.

Because he'd read the words she'd written. He'd returned her story to her office and noticed it had disappeared from her desk. He'd sat in her chair in her home office and imagined her writing there, having sexy dreams about him.

He lifted his head and rubbed his thumb over her lower lip. Touching her was an addiction. A craving that never really left him.

"Tell me," he said again.

She wrapped her small hand around his wrist, turned her face into his hand, breathing deeply and keeping her eyes closed.

"They are pictures of... Well, I don't spend a lot of holidays with my father and those are photos taken with other people's families."

He felt a punch in his gut. She had more hidden depths than he'd realized and he had no idea if he knew how to sort them out. Why did he even want to?

The answer was simple and easy. He wanted to be her hero. He wanted to be worthy of the fantasies she'd weaved about him. He wanted to be the kind of man she'd still look up to when she knew him well.

Instead, he was stuck with being the man he'd always been. Someone who took one look around him when the going got rough and then packed his bags and looked for a different challenge. One that wasn't personal. One that didn't really affect him.

But it was too late where Grace was concerned. He liked the personal connection they had.

She watched him with her wide, sad eyes, waiting for him to say something.

"No one's life is picture perfect," he said, trying to share with her what he'd learned in the last fifteen years. How he'd struggled to come to terms with having his entire life turn out to be a lie. Not a malicious one, but a lie nonetheless.

"I don't want perfection," she said. She shifted away from him, wrapping her arms around her own waist.

He didn't want her to soothe herself when he was right there and more than willing to offer her comfort. He wrapped his arm around her shoulder and pulled her into his body.

"I've got to go to the restroom," she said.

He guessed she was just using it as an excuse but got to his feet. "I'll show you where they are."

Adam was easy to follow as they moved through the arena hallway toward the restrooms. Since this was a Platinum Club floor there wasn't a lot of foot traffic. She knew asking to go to the bathroom was lame and had avoidance written all over it, but Adam had been pushing too hard and she was about to just give in and tell him another one of her secrets. Peel away another layer of her carefully crafted facade and bare her soul.

She didn't want to get into a heavy conversation. She'd been having fun. Having a normal date and, somehow, she'd blundered and ruined it.

"You don't have to wait for me. I can find my way back to the box."

"I don't mind."

She ducked into the ladies' room. When she came back out she glanced around for him. The hallway was a little more crowded now. For a second she couldn't find him and wondered if he'd gone back without her. She started that way when she felt his heavy hand on her shoulder. He drew her to a stop.

"I'm not going to stop asking you questions about those pictures."

"I'm making it into too big a deal. Really it's nothing. A group of teachers and I have a wine and supper club. There are twelve of us and we take turns hosting the monthly dinner. The last time they were at my place someone commented on the fact that I had no family snapshots anywhere."

"So you started displaying photos taken with other people's families?"

"Yes. Until then, I never noticed that I didn't have any photos and other people had them. I'm not one for looking back."

"Yet you crave roots."

"That's different. I just want to have a place I belong. I don't need decades of ancestry for that."

A couple brushed past them, oblivious to the world. They had their arms around each other. She realized it would be easy to look at them and assume life was simple for them—and maybe it was.

She always wanted relationships to fall into nice, straightforward categories. The work relationships she had with Bruce and the teachers on her staff. The mentoring role she had with her students. But she couldn't put an easy label on Adam. She wanted him more than she'd ever wanted any man.

It was a weakness to want him. Because he didn't fit into the safe boxes that others did and she had the feeling he never would. He was never going to be someone she felt completely comfortable with.

"Let's go back to our box," he said, cupping his hand under her elbow and leading her back to the stairs. She couldn't read his expression but had the distinct impression that he was angry.

"Adam?"

They stopped walking and turned. Grace wanted to groan out loud when she saw Sue-Ellen Hanshaw. Of course she always looked well put-together and made Grace feel every bit the small-town poor kid she'd always been.

She suspected the other woman didn't do it intentionally. Sue-Ellen definitely put her kids and family first, which Grace could admire.

"Hi, Sue-Ellen, enjoying the game?"

"I am. I thought I saw you earlier with Grace."

Wasn't she clever?

"Adam was just giving me a quick lesson in hockey."

"Where are you two sitting?" Sue-Ellen asked.

"Up in one of the private boxes." Adam's tone didn't broker an invitation to join them.

"Do you have other guests?"

Sue-Ellen sounded suspicious. With each question Grace felt her skin get tighter. She wanted to disappear—heck, if she hadn't been running away from Adam's questions, they'd never have seen Sue-Ellen.

"No. It's just the two of us," Adam said.

"Is that wise?"

"We've been discussing the school," Grace said quickly. "Did you hear Adam has arranged for a few celebrities to come play in the charity basketball tournament to raise money for the school's gym?"

Sue-Ellen smiled and the expression almost reached her eyes. "Thank you, Adam, for doing that."

"It was no problem. To be honest, it was Christian's idea."

Sue-Ellen's son was one of the many students who were working hard to keep the school going.

"I think he had an ulterior motive. He's a huge Bottle Rocket fan," Sue-Ellen said, naming one of the bands on Adam's record label. She was being friendly, but Grace sensed disapproval under the surface.

Grace knew practically his entire artist base thanks to some time spent on the Internet. She wasn't surprised to hear that Sue-Ellen's son, a junior, had come up with the idea. She wondered if Sue-Ellen realized how badly her son wanted the school to stay open. If she knew how much the changes in their personal lives over the last two years had affected her son.

"It was a great suggestion," Grace said.

Sue-Ellen flushed at the compliment to her son. "I'm so impressed at the way he's gotten involved with saving the school."

"You should be proud of him," Adam said.

"I am. I'll see you both at the meeting on Thursday, right?"

"Yes," Grace said. "I'm looking forward to hearing all the parents' ideas."

Sue-Ellen moved on. Adam made no move to go back to the box to watch the rest of the game.

"Are you embarrassed to be seen with me?" he asked, pulling her out of the walkway and into the shadows.

"No. Why would you think that?" she asked. Her back was against the wall. He leaned closer to her, putting one arm on either side of her head, caging her with his body. She put her hand on his chest to keep him from coming any closer. Because she wanted more than anything to say to hell with Sue-Ellen and Malcolm and the morality patrol and just give in to the temptation that was Adam.

"Your comments to Sue-Ellen made it seem like we weren't on a date," he said, canting his hips forward so that he was nestled against the center of her body. Flashes of light flickered in from the arena. Or was that her, reacting to him?

"Good. The last thing we need is for anyone to know

that you and I are dating. That's the kind of publicity the school doesn't need," she said. Even to her own ears, her voice sounded breathless.

"Why good? This feels like a date to me, Gracie."

She was mesmerized by the latent passion in his eyes and leaned up toward him. Brushed her lips over his once and then again. She had never had a man so completely take over every part of her life before. She suspected that Adam didn't even know that he was doing it.

He kept his lips out of reach. "Explain to me about Sue-Ellen."

"She's reporting everything I do to Malcolm."

"I didn't realize it was that bad. You don't have to pretend we aren't dating."

"Are we dating?"

"I think I just said we were."

"We've only had dinner once. And now, the game. It's not like we've really had a chance to get to know one another."

"We know each other intimately," Adam said, wrapping his arms around her and pulling her fully into his body. He lowered his head and brushed his lips over hers. "Don't we, Grace?"

She knew he was asking her something important, but she couldn't think or answer. She just wanted to lose herself in this moment and in this man. *This* was what she'd been wanting when she put those photos on her mantel, snapshots of a life that wasn't really her own. She'd always craved this. This, what she felt right now with Adam.

And she knew exactly what *this* was. A feeling of belonging and acceptance that had been missing all of her life.

Adam lifted his head after a long moment had passed. He drew her out of the shadows, leading her down the hallway and toward the exit. "Let's get out of here."

Adam parked his car at the curb in front of Grace's house. A quiet had fallen between them as they'd left American Airlines Center. He didn't know what to say to her, unusual for him. He usually had no problem filling awkward silences with small talk. But he and Grace had somehow moved beyond small talk and now he had nothing to say. No way to communicate with words. The charm that he usually employed with women wasn't going to be enough.

She watched him with her wide, wounded eyes and he knew that he couldn't leave her. Not tonight, he told himself, but a part of him recognized that as a lie.

"Thanks for taking me to the game," she said in that quiet, polite way of hers.

"It was my pleasure. I'd like to take you out again tomorrow night," he said, stretching his arm along the back of her seat. She tipped her head to the side.

"I could make us dinner at my place."

"I'd like that. I'll bring the wine."

She smiled at him and for a moment he felt something that he hadn't realized had been missing in his life. A sense of total normalcy. Like they *were* just two people dating. Like there were no secrets between them. No lies that were quietly waiting to jump out.

On one level it angered him because he knew that the lies were his own and having been on the other side, having been the person who'd been lied to, he knew how much that was going to hurt. Unless he could figure out a way to make Grace tell him about the erotic story. Her fantasy of being his mistress.

"What's your dream date?" he asked.

She quirked one of her eyebrows at him and licked her lower lip. "Something like tonight, I guess."

"You guess?" he asked, flirting with her. Finding his rhythm in the new, easy way she held herself. This was something he knew how to do.

"Yeah, I guess."

"Are you going to invite me in for a nightcap?"

She gathered her purse from the floor and opened it pulling out her keys. "I wasn't planning on it."

"Come on, Gracie. I want to hear what you'd change about tonight." He turned off the car and leaned back in the seat to watch her, his hand stretched over the back of her headrest. Her flowery perfume filled the air, and when she moved her head strands of her hair rubbed over his wrist. He wanted to wrap his hand in her hair to not have to play the waiting game that dating couples did. Instead he wanted to claim her, to throw her over his shoulder and take her to bed.

In her fantasies he already had. Even in his own, he'd claimed her. He wanted her with a bone-deep fascination that made everything else pale. He needed to be inside her silky curvy body, marking her as his own. Finding a way to bind her to him. He didn't understand the need, didn't want to question it too closely. He only knew that he wanted Grace.

"Why?" she asked.

He didn't want to have to explain himself. Didn't want to have to come up with more reasons to drag this conversation out until she felt comfortable enough to invite him into her home. "So I can better plan next time."

"What if you're the thing I'd change?" she asked, a saucy grin on her face.

She knew what she was doing. She was playing him to see how much he would take. He had the suspicion that this was new to her—flirting with a man, finding her feet with him—so he tugged on a strand of her hair and brought her face closer to his.

"Then you're out of luck. I'm not going anywhere."

The words resonated inside him and he realized that he wanted to stay with her. To stay as long as he could.

She watched him with those wide, serious eyes and then said, "Not even in the house for a drink?" She opened her door and stepped out of the car.

He watched her for a moment. Something had changed from earlier. There was more confidence in the way she moved. As if she knew he was going to follow her. And he was. He was going to follow her and give her a night straight out of her dreams.

Grace was sure and competent and very in charge in real life, but in her fantasy she wanted a man to dominate her. To take control of her passion. He followed her up her walk, pressing his remote to lock the doors on his car and set the alarm.

He followed her as if she'd promised him the answers to questions he'd always posed. And he knew she didn't have them. Knew that, like women or projects in the past, he wouldn't really find what he'd been chasing. He'd thought he'd found the answers before only to be disappointed.

But tonight none of that mattered. All that he cared about was that she'd invited him in. She'd made a move in real life, not just in her written fantasies, and that was good enough for him.

She had something he wanted and because he was a guy it was partially tied up in lust for her curvy body. But he knew there was more to it than lust.

She led him into her house and got them both a glass of wine, a California merlot that was full-bodied and fruity. She sat on one edge of her couch, leaving plenty of space between the two of them.

"I thought we were beyond this," he said, quietly. She blew hot and cold with him, one minute flirty and sexy as hell, the next retreating behind her walls. Watching him with those enigmatic eyes of hers that made him realize he might never know any of her secrets.

"Beyond what?"

"This space between us," he said.

She took a sip of her wine. "Whenever I think about you here with me, I can't help thinking—what is this man doing with *me?*"

"I'm here because you make the world come alive for me."

"That sounds hokey."

"I know. But I can't think of any other way to describe it."

"Your life is pretty exciting without me in it."

"No, Grace, it isn't. My life is full of events and people, but it's all routine. I learned a long time ago that routine is important to survival."

"Routine is getting up at six every morning, eating cereal and driving to work. Routine is not spending your day surrounded by rock stars and celebrities."

"I guess it just depends on your perspective," he said quietly. Thinking about how one little detail could change a life. The lies his parents had told had changed his life. The story of Grace's he'd read had changed their lives. And though he knew he needed to say something, to somehow reveal the secret he was keeping, he still wasn't able to find the right words.

Eight

"Where were we?" he asked, his voice a sexy whisper in her ear.

He nudged her center and she shifted against him, trying to get even closer. It was impossible with the layers of cloth between them. Her skirt was hiked up, but not enough.

"I think we were here," she said, looking down at her bare breasts.

"Show me where I left off," he said.

She drew his head down to her lips. He kissed his way down her neck and bit lightly at her nape. She shuddered, clutching at his shoulders, pressing her body harder against him. He bent his head and his tongue stroked her nipple.

Excerpt from "Adam's Mistress" by Stephanie Grace

Adam looked like he belonged in her house as he sat next to her on the couch. A part of her was afraid she was building too much around him and their relationship the same way she did with those photos of her with other people's families on the mantel. Creating the illusion that there was more to her life than there really was.

He spread his arms along the back of the sofa, his body open and relaxed. She thought about the story she'd written. The story that, for her, was bold and erotic. A fictional account that she used to fill the empty part of her life. The part that she'd always really been afraid to admit that she wanted.

But she and Adam had already made love once. She'd already had an orgasm in his arms and watched him have one next to her. They'd been intimate in a way—

"What are you thinking so hard about?"

She shrugged. What could she say to him that wouldn't make her sound…like herself? Like the scared and insecure woman she was deep inside?

"Nothing," she said, wanting to believe that it was strategy and not fear of rejection that held her still on her side of the couch.

"If it doesn't feel right don't do it," he said, a wry grin on his face. But the expression seemed forced.

She guessed he was experiencing something similar to what she felt. She skimmed her gaze down his body, stopping when she noticed his erection. She hadn't even touched him, how could he be aroused by her?

"I guess you can tell how much I like you," he said, gesturing to his body.

"Why?"

He turned to her then, putting one hand on her face, his fingers gentle as he traced the line of her cheekbones. But when he started to speak she put her fingers over his lips. She didn't want to hear what he had to say. Whatever expectations he had of her, she didn't want to know them. Didn't want her fears of living up to what he wanted to stop her.

"Forget I asked. I like you, too."

"Show me," he said.

Grace pushed all her doubts from her mind about why Adam was here. He *was* here, and that was enough for her. She wasn't going to waste the opportunity to be with him. Not like the last time at his house in the shower, when she'd wanted to reach for him again but had stopped herself. Her fantasies, which had fed her secret life, paled in comparison to the real thing.

How could the imagined feel of his hand on the back of her neck match the actual warmth and weight of the real thing?

He watched her steadily, awareness of him growing in her until she had to lean forward and capture his lips with hers. His mouth was firm and hard. He didn't open his lips, just waited to see how far she'd take it. She brushed her mouth back and forth over his.

She licked at his lips before using her teeth to draw his lower lip into her mouth, scraping her teeth over the plump flesh. She rested her hands on his shoulders for balance as she leaned over him. The angle forced his head back so that she was in complete control.

He moaned and pulled her down on his lap, shifting the balance of power in that one move. He took control, his hands sliding up to hold her head still as he plundered the depths of her mouth.

She shifted her legs so that she straddled his hips. She lifted her head and stared down at him. His eyes were narrowed and intense as he looked up at her.

"Take off your T-shirt."

"Only if you take off your shirt."

He nodded. She sank back on his thighs, reaching for the waistband of her shirt. She pulled it up over her head and then held it awkwardly in front of her for a minute. She knew what her body looked like with just jeans on. Her white belly was visible. Some of her skin swelled over the waistband.

He unbuttoned his shirt and pushed it off his shoulders. He was lean and ripped with rock-hard, defined muscles that a businessman shouldn't have. "You work out."

"Yeah, I get restless and no matter where I am there's always a gym."

"There are also bars and women."

"That's not who I really am, Gracie. Why are you holding on to that shirt?"

She shrugged. No way was she going to say something derogatory about her body when she had him half-naked and wanting her. She pushed her concerns from her head and focused instead on Adam.

She dropped her shirt and his hands were on her immediately. His fingers traced the lines of her torso before sliding around her back and up her spine. He found the back clasp of her bra and she felt him undo it. He left the fabric on her, continuing his path up her back to her neck.

He drew her forward, his mouth meeting hers again. Making her forget the lingering doubts she had. There was no room in her mind for anything but Adam when he touched her.

His hands kept moving while his mouth held hers captive. He swept her bra aside and then pressed between her shoulders until her breasts were against his naked chest.

Her breath caught in her throat and she closed her eyes, wanting to capture this moment forever. Wanting to never forget the way he felt against her.

He lifted his head, skimming his mouth down her jaw to her neck. He nibbled on her skin, making her feel like a meal being offered up to him. His hands and his mouth made her come alive in his arms.

Her nipples tightened as his fingers drew near them but he only skimmed the fleshy part of her breasts and then moved downward to the swell of skin above the waistband of her jeans. He traced the seam where fabric and skin met all the way around to her back where the jeans gaped away from her body.

He dipped his finger down, touching the silky fabric of her panties and then slipping underneath to caress the sensitive skin at the base of her spine. She shifted in his arms as his mouth moved down her neck.

He sucked on the pulse beating at the base of her neck. She felt an answering pull from the center of her body. She shifted on his lap, rubbing her center over his erection.

He groaned deep in his throat, his finger on her back caressing the cleft in her buttocks. She canted her hips away from that unfamiliar touch as his mouth moved lower, finding her nipple and kissing it.

"You have very pretty breasts, Gracie."

She didn't know what to say to that. She could barely think coherently while her body was in this state of need—aching need—and chaos.

He kept his one hand in the back of her jeans and drew the other one down her body, tracing her face and then her neck, lingering on the spot where he'd sucked on her skin, then going right between her breasts. He didn't stop there, kept tracing a line down the center of her body. He flicked open the snap of her jeans and lowered the zipper so he could keep touching her.

She had braced her hands on his shoulders and sank back on his thighs so that she didn't have to use her hands for balance. She scraped her nails down his chest. She loved the muscled steel of him.

The light dusting of hair on his chest tickled her fingers. She lowered her head to taste his skin, licking delicately at him before nipping him with her teeth. His hands tightened on her, his fingers finding one nipple and pinching her lightly.

He tangled his fingers in her hair and drew her head up to his. Both of his hands slipped down to her breasts as he rotated his palms over her. She lost herself in a wave of feeling as he drew her forward, urging her up on her knees.

"Offer your breasts to me," he said in a gravelly voice.

Nerves assailed her for a minute and she was stuck in that place where she came up against what she'd never done and what she wanted to do. This was almost exactly what she'd fantasized when she'd written her story. The fire in Adam's eyes and the heat between her legs convinced her not to back down.

She cupped herself and leaned forward. The line between reality and fantasy blurred. She felt the Grace Stephens she'd always been drop away and the Grace Stephens she'd always wanted to be take center stage.

Her eyes met Adam's and he watched her with that level, steady gaze of his filled with passion and heat. A shiver of awareness slid down her spine. She aroused him. She made him want her. It was a heady feeling and she savored it.

She tipped her head to the side, enjoying the feel of her hair sliding over her shoulders. "Taste me."

"With pleasure," he said.

He kept one hand at the small of her back, urging her forward. Dropping kisses along the tops of her breasts, tracing the lines of her fingers with his tongue before suckling her nipple deep into his mouth. She let go of her breasts and grabbed his shoulders for support as the entire world tipped on its axis.

Everything narrowed down to the two of them. To his mouth on her breast, his hand on her back sliding lower and pushing her down against his erection. She wished she'd taken off her jeans.

Reaching between their bodies, she caressed his hard length though the fabric of his pants. Everything he did turned her on.

He suckled her breast and urged her to rock her hips against him. She felt the weight of her hair against her back and, as she leaned forward into his body, she felt him surround her. She felt cherished, safe, wanted in a way that awakened the hidden woman inside her.

She arched into his touch, felt him everywhere. His hands touching and caressing her, driving her to the edge. His mouth and teeth nibbling at her breasts until they felt too full, too heavy. She needed more. Needed something from him that she couldn't find.

She rocked against him, her nails digging into his shoulders as everything inside her tightened. Every nerve ending she had was so sensitized to the slightest brush of him against her that she felt herself close to the edge.

"Are you close?"

"Yes…."

"Come for me," he said, touching her intimately. The pressure pushed her over the edge. Everything in her body clenched down and she rocked against him.

She held his head to her body as waves washed over, leaving her shivering in his arms. He pushed to his feet, holding her high in his arms and walked down the hallway to her bedroom.

Adam tried not to analyze what he felt as he walked into Grace's bedroom with her in his arms. She was so wonderfully responsive to his every touch that she made him feel like the king of the world. The king of her world, really. The only man who existed for her.

He felt almost as if, for the first time, he knew who he really was. That Adam Bowen wasn't a fraud.

Tonight, when they were at the hockey game, he'd realized that her attention never wandered from him. That she didn't want to be with anyone else.

And when she let him make love to her, he had her trust whether she wanted to admit it or not.

He set her down in the center of her bed. The head of the bed was covered in pillows. Only the light from the hallway spilled into the room. Not enough. He wanted to see more of Grace.

He reached over to turn on the lamp on her nightstand.

"What are you doing?" she asked.

"Making sure every detail is right."

"Here in my room?"

"Yes."

"Why?"

"We're only going to have one first time together. I want it to be everything you've ever imagined it would be."

"I can't imagine anything better than you in my arms, Adam."

His heart ached a little. There it was again. That sweet honesty that made him remember he knew more about her fantasies than she would want him to. Knowing that made it easier for him to keep his control though he was rock hard. Knowing he was going to fulfill them made his spine tingle.

He unsnapped his jeans and pushed them down his legs. He'd forgotten his shoes and had an awkward moment where he had to bend over to remove them.

He felt the butterfly-light touch of her hand on the back of his thigh. Her fingers explored him while he was doubled over. He got his shoes and socks off and pushed his jeans to the floor.

Standing there in just his jockey shorts he let her explore him. Her fingers traced the line of a scar he'd always had, which wrapped from the front of his hip around to his back.

"How'd you get this?"

Adam shrugged. His mother had told him it had happened when he was only six months old. She'd never said anything more and he'd never asked about it. But when he'd learned that she was really his adoptive mother he'd wondered again how he'd gotten the scar.

"I've always had it," he said. She traced it again with her fingers then hooked her other arm around his waist and drew him back to the edge of the bed. He felt her lips along his flank. Kissing and nibbling, tasting him. He tightened painfully and he knew that the slow and easy round of lovemaking he'd wanted for their first time wasn't going to happen.

He wanted her. He needed her soft touches. He needed her combination of shy looks and bold caresses. He needed…her. He sank down on the bed, moving over her.

She smiled up at him, her hands still exploring him everywhere. Touching his chest, tangling in the hair there and tugging on it.

He pushed her jeans down her legs, removing her shoes and socks, too. He sank back on his haunches and just stared at her. She was bare except for the brief fabric of her bright blue bikini panties. They were made of silk and lace and he remembered the feel of her warmth against his fingers, the fabric under his hand as he'd touched her on the couch.

He wanted more than memory. He wanted to feel her again. To feel her now. "Are you on the pill?"

"No. I don't have any condoms, either."

"I brought my own."

"Always prepared?" she asked. There was something in her tone that made him realize the answer to this next question was very important.

"I'm prepared for you. I don't carry condoms around as a rule but you are pure temptation, Gracie, and I knew I wouldn't be able to resist."

"Come to me," she said, leaning back against the pile of pillows. She pushed her panties down her hips and kicked them to the floor. She opened her arms and bent her knees.

He shed his underwear in record time and grabbed the condom from his pocket. He'd put it there earlier in the hopes that the evening would end this way.

He took her feet in each of his hands and drew her down until she lay flat on the bed. He pushed her legs wide open and held himself over her, braced on his forearms leaving only an inch of space between their bodies.

He lowered his hips and felt her moist center. His control slipped. She shifted, reaching down to encircle him with her hand.

"Where's your condom?"

"Right here." He dropped it next to her. He kissed her, starting at her neck and moving down her body, unable to resist the temptation to taste her. He leaned down to lick each nipple until it tightened. Then he blew gently on the tips. She raked her nails down his back.

He held her still with a hand on her stomach as he suckled on each of her breasts until her nipples were hard and red. He glanced up at her and saw her swallow. Her hands shifted on the bed next to her hips.

He traced a path down her center until he got to her belly button. He loved the small mound of her belly. He kissed her flesh there then moved lower, dipping his fingers into the warm moisture in her center.

"Adam, please."

She took his hard length in her hand and followed with her tongue, teasing him with quick licks and light touches.

He arched on the bed, thrusting up before he realized what he was doing. He pulled her away from his body, wanting to be inside her.

He pulled her up to his body until she straddled his hips. He fumbled for the condom, finding it a few feet from them, then ripping the packet open with one hand.

He sheathed himself and then, using his grip on her hips, he pulled her down and slipped into her body. With one quick movement, he rolled them over to take command.

She arched her back, reaching up to entwine her arms around his shoulders. He thrust harder, slid deeper still into her, and felt every nerve in his body tense. Reaching between their bodies he touched her between her legs until he felt her body start to tighten around him.

He let himself go in a rush, continuing to thrust into her until his body was drained. He then collapsed on top of her, laying his head between her breasts.

A feeling of contentment started to wash over him. But Grace's soft sigh and the emotions coursing through him made him tense. There was a wealth of caring in that sigh and in the arms that wrapped trustingly around him. How would she feel when she realized the man she'd honored with her body and let past her guard, the man who claimed to hold the truth in highest regard, had been lying to her?

Nine

"I need you, Grace."
She took his jaw in her hands and pulled his face
up to hers. His pupils were dilated, and between
her legs she felt him, hot and hard.
"I need you, too."

Excerpt from "Adam's Mistress" by Stephanie Grace

Grace rolled over, glancing at the clock. Three a.m.
Too early for the alarm, but something had woken her.
She shifted in the bed and encountered Adam. He was
warm and solid. *Real.*

Her thighs ached and her breasts were tender from
making love with him, but she didn't mind. She liked
the feeling being possessed by him left in her. She

realized she'd forgotten about the scents and smells of sex when she'd written her story about Adam.

Adam moved in his sleep, rolling from his side to his back. She shifted up on her elbow and tried to see him in the darkened room. Tried to make out the features of this man who'd made her realize that she'd been half asleep until he'd come into her life a few weeks ago.

But she couldn't. He didn't snore and other than that movement he was a pretty solid sleeper. She rested one hand on his chest, lightly, just over his heart. She felt it beating under her palm. She wanted to lay her head on his chest, but didn't want to wake him.

Didn't want to have to endure him holding her until he thought she was asleep before he slipped away. Just the way Dean had the few nights they'd spent together. She'd only slept with him a few times, unable to bear having been so close physically to someone who didn't want her to touch him unless they were having sex.

"Gracie?"

"Hmm?"

"What are you doing way over there?" he asked.

"Trying not to disturb you."

He moved his arm, wrapping it around her waist and drew her next to him on the bed. Her breasts pressed to the side of his chest and her head came to rest on his shoulder. He tangled his hand in her hair, something she realized he did a lot. Wrapping his fingers in her curls, he tipped her head back.

"I like having you next to me."

Sleepily he found her mouth with his and then gently

guided her head down to his chest. His hand on her back swept up and down her spine as he anchored her to him.

Sex, she thought. It was okay, really it was.

"You smell and feel so good, Gracie. I'm almost afraid to wake up and find I dreamed you." He tucked her even closer to his side.

No man had ever held her as closely as Adam held her now. She tried to tell herself not to read too much into the embrace but when he held her like this he felt solid, real. Like the very thing she'd been searching for.

When she'd written the story "Adam's Mistress," she'd focused on the physical details of what making love with him would be like. How it would feel to have his masculine attention turned on her.

She hadn't let herself hope that some kind of caring or affection would be there on his side. She just wasn't the kind of woman who inspired that in men. Her father had been the first one to teach her that lesson and Dean had followed it up. But Adam made her feel like she wasn't the kind of woman that men left.

This spot on his chest, right over his heart, seemed to be made for her head. It was the perfect place for her to rest. His hand in her hair, caressing her, made her feel wanted in a way that nothing else had in a long time. No, she thought, she'd never felt wanted like this before.

She was afraid to believe that this thing with Adam could be more than just a short-term relationship. The complications she'd made for herself by lying here in his arms were too many to count.

But she didn't care anymore. She'd gladly take on the challenge for more nights like this one.

She should sleep but couldn't. Nighttime was always when she was plagued with doubts and fears of the future. Nighttime was when she remembered vividly the words her father had said to her in his quiet, preaching voice as she'd packed her bags and left his house at age sixteen.

Nighttime was the one time when she was truly alone with all the ghosts of her mistakes. And she'd never liked it.

Nighttime had also always been her time for dreaming—and for the past three years, those dreams had been of Adam Bowen.

Now he was here and she should be sleeping blissfully. But she couldn't. What was it about her that could never just be happy? Never just be content with what she had? Why did she always want more?

And she did want more from Adam. As nice as this was, she wanted him to wake up and tell her…oh, man, this was pathetic. She'd only really known the man for a few weeks but she wanted him to be in love with her.

She wanted him to somehow realize what they could have together and be the embodiment of her fantasy Adam. The one she'd never been able to make commit to her on the pages she wrote. And the one she'd wanted to.

She turned away from Adam. Unable to lie there in the dark with her mind so full of those thoughts and her heart so full of longing that it felt like it might really break. And not because of anything that Adam did, but because of what she'd always wanted.

Adam followed her, his arms staying around her. She felt his mouth against her neck as he pulled her back against his body.

"What is it?" he asked.

She couldn't think for a minute of what to say or do. She could only feel a bittersweet mixture of hope and realism as he held her. He was naturally affectionate and it was going to be so hard to keep herself from falling in love with him.

No sooner had the words formed in her mind than she realized it was already too late. That she did love Adam. She'd been half in love with him from the moment they'd met and getting to know the man behind the fantasy had left her vulnerable to herself.

"Gracie?"

She smiled at the way he said her name. She'd always been too serious to be a Gracie but somehow Adam saw her differently.

"Nothing's wrong. Just a bad dream."

Adam woke a little after six, surprised he'd slept so soundly. But then Grace seemed to calm the chaotic, restless part of his soul. That knowledge took him aback and made him want to analyze it. But he wasn't good at looking for answers to emotional questions. That was why he'd spent so much time avoiding Plano and the school his family had started.

He remembered her waking in the middle of the

night and knew that she probably wasn't used to a man sleeping with her. He wasn't really used to sleeping with a woman in his bed. But he always stayed the night even though he usually found it difficult to get a good night's sleep. He was sensitive enough to know that no woman wanted a man she'd just had sex with to sneak out while she was sleeping, however much he wanted to go.

He didn't want to with his Grace.

The morning sunlight spilled through the small cracks in the plantation blinds. The ones on the top of the window had been left open and the light was moving across the floor toward the bed.

He glanced down at Grace, aware that he wanted to make promises. Promises that the past had proven he couldn't keep. Vowing to always be there to hold her in the darkest part of the night and keep her bad dreams at bay. Pledging that she'd never want for anything again. Assuring her and himself that the lonely restlessness that had always plagued him and, he suspected, her would never haunt either of them again.

But those were words he couldn't form. No matter that it felt right to have Grace in his arms. To sleep in her embrace through the long night. He was afraid to let go of the past long enough to believe that this woman in his arms could be the future.

Because he knew that security was the ultimate illusion. His parents' death had been the first time he realized that there was no such thing as a safety net. Learning the truth of his birth had confirmed it. And

every relationship he'd had since then had simply rein-
forced those beliefs.

He hated that about himself. Knew that it stemmed
from the darkest part of his own fears—fears that he
usually only examined when he was out getting drunk
with Stevie Taylor of Viper. The two of them ques-
tioned why money couldn't buy happiness.

He looked down at Grace's fragile features, her face
soft and relaxed in slumber. All the money in his bank
accounts didn't mean a thing to her. He'd read her secret
fantasies, he knew that as far as she was concerned it
was the man who made the difference. Not his finances.

A part of him was soothed by that. The twenty-five-
year-old guy who'd learned that the legacy he thought
he'd been entitled to was a sham liked the fact that this
woman wanted him, not the Bowen name.

Damn, he was getting maudlin. He closed his eyes,
burying his face against the back of her neck, in those
soft curls of hers that he couldn't get enough of
touching. She shifted in his arms, her backside brushing
his morning erection, and he groaned deep inside.
Wanting her again. After last night he should be well
sated for at least 24 hours, but he knew with Grace
nothing was the way it usually was.

He'd never get enough of caressing her soft curves.
Of making love to her. He canted his hips forward,
nestling himself in the curves of her buttocks. She shifted
in his arms, rubbing her back against his chest, moving
until they were pressed together from shoulder to thighs.

One of his hands was nestled between her breasts

and he shifted it to cup her right one. He held her in his palm, forefinger caressing the soft weight of her. He liked the textures of her body.

He pushed the covers off them so he could see her. Her skin was smooth and creamy, her breasts topped with pretty dark pink nipples. His hand looked big and dark against her pale skin. He used his thumb and finger to caress her nipple until it hardened under his touch.

Her legs moved restlessly against him. He wedged his thigh between hers and felt her heat on his leg. He used his other hand to hold her to him low at her stomach, one finger snaking lower to caress the small bud at the center of her body.

"Adam…"

Her voice was sleepy and husky and he knew what she wanted. Knew that he'd brought her from sleep into a world of aching need. That suited him, because he ached for her. He needed her in ways that he hoped she'd never realize.

"Hmm…"

She rocked her hips against him until his erection was poised at the damp opening of her body. He wanted to thrust into her just like this. Forget about the future or the consequences of taking her totally naked.

But he knew better. He didn't want Grace to have to confront an unwanted pregnancy. He shifted around on the bed, leaving her for a minute to get another condom out of the pocket of his pants.

He sheathed himself and came back to her. Pulled her back against him. She shifted around until she was where she'd been before, her right leg draped over his hip, her breast nestled in his hand.

"Look at me," he said.

She tipped her head back against his shoulder, her eyes slumberous. He leaned down and took her mouth, thrust his tongue deep inside her. He guided himself to her opening, then plunged into her with one steady thrust. She gently nipped his tongue and thrust her own back into his mouth. He held her tightly to him as he slid hilt deep into her body before pulling all the way out. He dropped kisses down the side of her neck, biting lightly at the pulse that beat steadily at its base as he thrust back into her.

She rocked against him, tightening herself as he pulled out one more time. She drew his hand from her hip down to the center of her body. He pushed his finger into the curls at her mound, finding the sensitive bundle of her nerves between her legs.

He rubbed her as he plunged back into her body again and again. He sucked hard on her neck, she moaned deeply and he felt her tighten. Knew what that sound signaled. He shifted her over onto her back, lifted her hips and thrust harder into her until the world coalesced around the woman in his arms and they climaxed together.

And he knew that the vows and promises he wanted to make had already been made as he held her like this, because he couldn't imagine leaving her.

Grace had never made breakfast for any man other than her father. She'd pretty much avoided the meal since she didn't like to eat it. But Adam was a big guy and he obviously needed to eat, so here she was in the kitchen staring into her refrigerator. Trying to pretend this morning was like any other when she was still trying to calm down from the last time they'd made love.

Her body still tingled. She couldn't believe the way he'd held her. She forgot about trying not to fall for him. Forgot about not making this night—this relationship—into more than it was. Forgot that heartbreak was inevitable.

"What are you looking for?" Adam asked, coming up behind her. He wore only his slacks from last night. His hair was unruly.

"Something to make you for breakfast," she said over her shoulder.

"Why?" he asked, wrapping one arm around her waist and pulling her back against him.

"Because…" She tipped her head back to look up at him. He leaned down and kissed her. Sipped at her mouth like she was all he'd need to find sustenance. She opened her mouth for him, knowing that she couldn't possibly make love to him again but that her body was readying for him.

He arched one eyebrow at her. "You were saying?"

She had no idea what they'd been talking about…oh, yeah, breakfast. "You seem like the kind of man who'd want a hearty breakfast."

He smiled down at her. "I have worked up an appetite this morning and I do like breakfast."

She blushed at the thought of what he'd done to work

up an appetite. She knew it was silly and she wished she didn't react that way but this was all too new to her.

He kissed her again and this time it was tender and almost sweet. When he lifted his head, she stared at his moist lips.

"I knew it," she said, trying desperately to marshal her thoughts back in order.

"I'm not picky. What do you usually eat?"

"A cereal bar," she said, nibbling on her lower lip. There was nothing in the refrigerator except a six-pack of fat-free yogurt that might have expired. She searched past the take-out containers for something that might feed Adam.

He made a face. "That's not breakfast."

"I know. That's why I'm searching my fridge."

He pulled her away from the appliance and shut the door. He lifted her up on the countertop and stood between her legs. She wrapped her arms around his waist, holding him to her. Resting her head on his shoulder, she closed her eyes, happy for this moment just to savor being with him.

He held her for a long time, his hands moving on her back, his head resting on the top of hers. Then his stomach growled and she pulled back.

"We've got to find you something to eat," she said.

He looked chagrined by his growling stomach. "Do you like omelets?"

"Yes, but I don't even have a carton of Egg Beaters," she said, deciding that she'd have to go grocery shopping and keep some real food in her fridge before he came back again.

"Egg Beaters? Woman, they aren't even real eggs. I'll run out and get everything we need and make you breakfast."

She frowned at him. "I wanted to do it."

"Gracie, it's clear you're not a cook." There was a teasing note in his voice that she'd never heard before. She suspected Adam felt like she did. That this moment was a respite from their realities. A chance to drop their guards and be themselves. She knew it couldn't last. That sooner or later reality would intrude and they'd be forced back into the roles they both knew so well.

"That obvious?" she asked, tipping her head to the side.

"Well, your fridge is full of take-out containers and expired food. I'll make us breakfast."

She didn't like it and knew why. *She* wanted to take care of *him.* To give him something here, in her home, that he wouldn't find anywhere else. It was part of her fantasy to cook for him, but he was right—she wasn't a cook.

"I want to do this. I like taking care of you."

Those words had a profound impact on her deep inside. She knew that he meant *cooking* for her, but it felt somehow like more.

"I could go to the store with you," she suggested. She enjoyed being with him and she didn't want to be apart. Actually that made her feel a little weak but it wasn't because she couldn't function without him. It was because she wanted to spend as much time together as they could before he left.

"Okay."

Her phone rang. Adam reached over to grab the cordless unit and handed it to her. She glanced down at the caller ID and saw that it was Sue-Ellen Hanshaw. Reality, intruding big-time.

She answered the call. "Good morning, Sue-Ellen."

"Not really a good one, Grace."

Her stomach sank. "What's up?"

"Our school is in the paper again and it's not good. The headline calls us a hotbed of sexy encounters."

"Who is it this time?"

"You. You and Adam."

Ten

He growled deep in his throat and lowered his head to hers again. This time there was no gentle seduction but a full out taking of her mouth. He didn't mask what he wanted—he took. And she let him.

One of his hands left her waist and cupped her butt, pulling her closer until her mound rested against his hardness.

Grace threw her head back and moaned. His other hand slid up her leg, not stopping until he reached the center of her. She moaned again as his fingers skimmed the pulsating center of her desire.

Excerpt from "Adam's Mistress" by Stephanie Grace

Adam wrapped his arm around Grace's shoulder and pulled her close to his side. All of the color had left her face and he knew Sue-Ellen had delivered bad news.

"What's going on?" he asked her.

"Hold on, Sue-Ellen," she said, putting her hand over the mouthpiece. "There's a story about us in *The Dallas Morning News.*"

Crap. The last thing he needed was press, but he should have anticipated it. The society column gossips loved to talk about him. He could guess what the article said about the two of them, but he didn't want to. He needed to see the article. Find out exactly what they were up against.

"Do you get the paper delivered?"

"Yes."

"Tell Sue-Ellen we'll call her back once we know what the article said."

He left the kitchen and walked outside, finding the paper under the tree in her front yard. There were cheery yellow and blue daffodils planted around the base of the tree.

It underscored what he knew about Grace. That she'd put down roots here. That the closing of the school wasn't just about losing a job. It was about changing the life she'd worked hard to carve out for herself here.

He went back into her house, vowing to himself that he'd do whatever he had to keep her safe. To make this latest hiccup go away.

He went back inside, hesitating in the doorway of the kitchen when he saw her leaning against the counter staring out the back window. Her arms were wrapped around her waist and she seemed so alone. It was an almost palpable feeling.

Dammit, how could a morning that had been going so perfectly have turned into this? He cleared his throat so he didn't startle her, but she didn't even turn toward him.

Hell, this wasn't good. She was breaking his heart. Because he could tell from the way she was focused so deep inside that she'd experienced this kind of wrenching, world-wrecking situation before. Whereas he always rolled on down the road when it happened, she hunkered down and shored up her defenses.

He wondered how many times she'd faced this kind of situation. He hoped that this time he could be there for her. But he'd never stayed. Could he this time?

"Gracie."

She lifted her head, her eyes filled with fatigue and weariness and something else he couldn't define.

"Did you get the paper?"

He held it up, shaking it out of the plastic bag. He set the bag on the counter and walked toward her. He drew her onto the bench seat in her breakfast nook.

"Whatever is in here, we'll face it together."

She gave him a sad smile that made him angry. She expected him to leave her. To let her face whatever was in the paper by herself. He couldn't battle the ghosts of her past any more than she could take on his. But together they had to face what was happening now.

"Don't do this," he said, getting a little angry that she was giving up on him before she'd even let him fail. The hard part was, he expected to disappoint her. He'd been doing that steadily to people since his parents had died.

"Don't do what?" she asked, in that school-administrator voice of hers, making him feel like a senior who'd been caught pulling a prank.

But he was a grown man and he knew how to handle these kinds of situations. He dealt with temperamental artists and negative media all the time. "Act like I'm just saying words that I don't mean. I don't know who let you down in the past, but it wasn't me. Let me fail on my own before you look at me with disappointment."

She bit her lower lip and then touched his face with those long cold fingers of hers. "I'm sorry. I didn't mean to make you feel like I was disappointed in you. I'm not."

He wanted to crush her to him and give her the promises she needed. The ones that would clear the clouds from her eyes and make her stop trembling.

"Then why do you look like you're about to cry?" he asked.

She shook her head. Pushing against his chest she moved away from him. Put a few inches of space between them but the gap felt bigger. And he knew that crossing it was going to be a trial. Suddenly he wondered if it was worth it. Was she worth it?

He was fighting to save a school he didn't care about so that he could get to know this woman better. And what he'd found was incredible, a woman who had touched him in ways no one else ever had.

"It'll sound really stupid if I have to say it out loud," she said.

And he had his answer. Of course Grace was worth the effort.

"Then whisper it to me," he said, putting his arm around and tucking her up against his side. He liked the feeling of her there. He didn't question it, only knew that he wanted her by his side.

"I'm so tired of struggling for everything. I wanted our relationship and the school's future to just go smoothly, but we've been sneaking around and I should have expected this to happen."

He cupped her jaw and tipped her head back. He sipped at her lips, kissing her languidly like there wasn't an urgent matter waiting for them. Like time had stood still and their morning was still ideal. Like he could give her what she wished for.

"You're right. Sneaking around was a mistake."

The worst part was, he knew that her fantasy man would be able to do those things for her. But this was real life and it ticked him off that he wasn't going to measure up to what she needed from a man. Even though her other man was a romanticized version of himself.

Grace didn't want to read the article. The headline said it all: How Far Will She Go to Save the School? Once she saw the picture of her and Adam in the hallway outside the Platinum Club at the American Airlines Center, the photograph seemed cheap and tawdry.

The photographer had captured them after Sue-Ellen had left, when Adam had caged her between his big body and the wall. She was staring up at him with her heart in her eyes. She'd had no idea her emotions were so transparent when she looked at him.

It was impossible to see Adam's expression from the angle of the photograph. But his body language was easy to read. His hips were canted toward her. His head was lowered, their mouths a breath apart.

It was worse than she'd anticipated. Everyone was going to know immediately that they were involved in a relationship. Analytically she knew that the photo wasn't anywhere near as bad as the one that had been taken of Dawn O'Shea and her lover. But it wasn't good, and the article accompanying it was downright salacious. Malcolm was going to be all over this.

"It's not as bad as I feared."

"It's bad enough," she said.

"Don't be like that. I'll call Malcolm and then the newspaper."

"What are you going to tell the newspaper?"

"That we're dating and have been for a while. I have a great spin doctor who will come up with an angle to help promote the school."

She didn't like this side of Adam, but knew she should be thankful he was going to step in and take care of the problem this photo had generated. The thing was—she didn't want him to. As adverse as it seemed, she didn't want him to take on the problems of the school and solve them the way he described.

"What about truth?"

"I'm not going to lie, Grace. We've known each other for three years."

She didn't know why it bothered her, but it did. A big part of her was saying to just shut up but she couldn't. "You barely knew I was there for three years."

"And your point is?"

"Nothing. I don't have a point, except that you said the truth was important to you and what you're proposing is a gross exaggeration of the truth."

He put the paper down. "What's really going on here?"

She shook her head. How could she explain to him what she didn't understand herself? She knew it wasn't fair, but she'd expected Adam to live up to the pedestal she'd put him on. And seeing that he had feet of clay, that he was human and made mistakes just like her…. Well, it was a little too much like real life.

She didn't like that about herself. That she'd expected him to act the way her fantasy man would.

"Sorry. I'm not sure how to handle this. I was starting to believe that we were going to save the school."

He took her hand in his. She looked up at him, knowing now that she had little chance of keeping him from seeing the hope and anticipation in her eyes.

"Don't give up yet. This isn't anything other than a minor setback. And we've done nothing wrong or immoral."

"I don't think Malcolm will see it that way."

"I'll handle Malcolm."

"Thanks, but I'm the one who's responsible for the school's reputation."

He sat back in his seat. "You don't want me to fight your battles for you."

"No, I don't." He was too attuned to her. She'd let down her guard last night and now she regretted it. In the middle of the night it had been comforting to realize that he was with her, but this morning... This morning she saw the danger in having a man such as Adam around. He would take over every corner of her life. Until he moved on.

"Why not?" he asked. She could tell he wanted the conversation done so he could take action. Call Sue-Ellen, call Malcolm, bend them both to his will with charm or threats or however he operated. She didn't know what he'd use for the two of them because she was realizing that he changed his way depending on the person he dealt with. He had a gift for seeing into a person's soul.

She shook her head at him. There was no way she was going to tell him why she didn't want him fighting her battles. If she started talking about that she'd probably end up confessing that she was afraid that she'd become too dependent on him. Which was bound to freak him out.

She had to stop thinking like a woman who'd been caught with her lover, a man in a position to make decisions about her own job. She had to be the administrator. The professional woman who knew how to handle a crisis.

"Let's not go into that. I better call Sue-Ellen back

and then call Malcolm." She scooted around the bench to get out.

Adam shackled her wrist in his big hand, holding her still. She glanced back at him, trying to figure out what he was doing.

"You're not calling anyone until you answer me."

"I don't answer to you, Adam." She tugged on her wrist but she couldn't budge it. "Let me go."

"Not yet."

Not yet. She knew he meant right this instant, but a part of her felt like those words summed up their relationship.

And she knew why she was so upset. Because when they'd been dating quietly, only the two of them had witnessed it. Now the world knew. Her world knew that she'd gone out with superstud Adam Bowen and if their relationship ended badly she'd have to spend the rest of her life dealing with pitying glances.

And she didn't want that. She'd left that behind in West Texas when she'd left the preacher and his sanctimonious ways.

She started struggling in a totally undignified way, needing to get away from him. Wanting to escape before she did something really stupid and begged him to not spin this situation. To just ignore it, even if it meant closing the school—anything that would leave her pride intact. But she didn't like what that said about her.

"Please, Adam. I need a minute to myself."

He held her for another second and then dropped her hand. "I'll be here, waiting for you."

* * *

Adam let her go because he knew he had no choice and he wasn't sure how to make her stay. He heard the shower come on and went into her bedroom, finding his BlackBerry on the floor near her bed.

Malcolm had called him twice. No matter that Grace wanted to handle the newspaper article, which was salacious and full of innuendo, he knew that he was responsible for this. The article added complications that he and Grace didn't need. But he wasn't really surprised by it. He should have anticipated that sooner or later a gossip columnist would find out he'd been spending time with Grace. And he planned to spend a lot more time with her.

He could get them to print a retraction and hope that would be enough to make things better for Grace. Only Adam knew that it wouldn't. He wanted to fill her life with all she'd missed. To somehow be her benefactor because it would insulate him from what he felt right now. From the pain of disappointing her.

He called Malcolm and got his voicemail. "It's Adam. We need to talk. Call me back."

He sat down on the bed to wait for her. Picked up the book she had lying on her nightstand and flipped through it. It was a romance novel. A business one in which the hero had come into the heroine's life for revenge but fell in love with her instead.

This was what Grace thought romance should be. He wanted to give it to her. He wanted to be her white knight, her hero. And a man who let his woman fight her own battles wasn't a hero.

She came out dressed in a large terrycloth robe, her hair wrapped in a towel. Her eyes were damp and he knew she'd been crying. He swallowed a curse.

He didn't know how to handle this. Should he keep the topic all business? Hell, he should just pull her into his arms and make love to her. Then the distance put between them by one phone call and one photo would disappear.

"I left a message for Malcolm. I'll take care of him. You can handle the parents since I don't have much contact with them."

She walked over to her dresser and opened a drawer, pulling out matching panties and bra in a light blue color. She held them in her hand. And he totally forgot what they were talking about.

All he could think of was how she'd look wearing only those small scraps of fabric. How the light blue would look against her creamy skin.

"That sounds like a good plan. The more I think about this, the more I think a clean break between the two of us will be the right solution," she said. Her words drew his mind away from his erotic daydream.

"I'm not ready for a break, Grace. I'm still getting to know you." He was still trying to unravel the many mysteries that were Grace. He hoped that she hadn't figured him out in such a short time. But he knew he wasn't that complicated. That he had no hidden depths for her to plumb. Just one secret that he kept to himself because he didn't know how to verbalize it.

"After you get to know me, will you be ready?" she asked, and he heard the hurt in her voice.

He shrugged his shoulders, unwilling to give her the words that would reassure her. He wasn't about to tell her that with the way she made him feel, he doubted he'd ever be ready to break up with her.

He wanted her in his life, but realistically didn't know how to make that happen. Articles like the one that had her so upset were a part of his life.

She made his fuller, gave him a different perspective…made him feel. And that had been missing since his parents died.

"We're so different, Adam. I thought that wouldn't matter, but I think it does."

"It doesn't matter," he said, pushing to his feet and going to her. There was no way he was letting her brush him off and push him out of her life. This was a minor problem. "I'm not going anywhere, Gracie."

The words crystallized everything for him. He didn't have the answers, but for once packing up and moving wasn't the most appealing route. He wanted to do whatever would make this work for him and Grace.

"Why not? It would be simpler for both of us if we just stopped seeing each other."

He thought about last night. And the last few weeks when they'd been working together. How his life had changed when he'd stumbled across an erotic story penned by her and knew that he couldn't go back to being the man he was before.

"I don't know what to say to you, Grace. But I do know that I can't let perception rule my life."

"Perception?"

"What other people think." He couldn't say more than that. Sometime he'd be able to tell her that he wasn't really who she thought he was, but not right now. Right now, he needed Grace.

He slowly unwrapped the towel from her head, dropping it to the floor. He held her face in both of his hands, lowered his head to hers and kissed her with all the emotions that he was afraid to identify.

She kept her hands between them. The satin fabric of the undergarments she still clutched felt cool and silky against his stomach. He wanted to crush her to him. To take her into his body so she couldn't get away. So that he could keep her safe from being hurt like she had been this morning.

He wanted to keep kissing her until time stood still and once again there were only the two them. He'd always been a practical person, but with Grace he wanted to be that fairy-tale hero.

He lifted her in his arms and carried her back to her bed, knowing that making love to her wasn't going to solve anything. Wasn't going to resolve any of the questions she had that he couldn't answer. Wasn't going to make the problems outside of her cozy little house go away.

But he needed her in the most basic and elemental way. He needed to feel her arms and legs wrapped around him. To feel her nails scratching down his back and her body melting around him.

Welcoming him into her embrace in a way that felt like forever. Because forever had just gotten a hell of a lot shorter than he'd expected it to be.

Eleven

He pulled his hips back, teased her with the promise of more. She shifted herself against his touch and finally felt him at the entrance of her body. He thrust deep inside her and she clutched at his shoulders.

His thumb rubbed at the center of her pleasure and the fire stormed through her, throwing her closer and closer to the pinnacle. Her breathing increased, she could scarcely catch her breath. His hand on her bottom held her hips steady as he rocked against her.

Excerpt from "Adam's Mistress" by Stephanie Grace

Grace walked into her office on Monday feeling a lot less confident than she had back in January when she thought the scandal of two teachers was going to close her school.

"Good morning, Bruce."

"Morning, Grace. Um, you've got a guest in your office."

"Who?"

"Dawn O'Shea."

Grace groaned. She'd been putting the fired teacher off but should have guessed that Dawn wouldn't let her do it indefinitely.

"This is really a bad time for her to be here."

"I know. That's why I put her in your office. Figured it was better if she was out of sight."

"Good thinking. I hate to ask this, but will you interrupt in five minutes?"

"No problem."

She entered her office. Dawn was standing behind Grace's desk staring out at the campus green. "I'm sorry I kept you waiting."

Dawn jerked around at the sound of Grace's voice. "We didn't have an appointment."

"Well, we have been trying to meet. I'm glad you stopped by, but today is going to be a little crazy."

"I saw the picture of you in the paper."

"Everyone did. What can I help you with?"

"I want my job back."

"It's too soon, Dawn. We're going to need at least another term before I can bring your name up to the board."

Dawn nodded. "I was afraid you'd say that."

"I wish there was something else I could do."

"Me, too," Dawn said, picking up her large brown leather purse and leaving.

This was really not what she needed. She made a mental note to contact the other administrators she knew in schools outside of Texas. Maybe one of them would have an opening for Dawn.

She was tired. Adam had left Saturday afternoon and she hadn't seen him since. He'd called a couple of times, but she'd refused to pick up the calls. The full board was meeting that afternoon and she needed to appear before them feeling fresh and strong. On her own.

But she'd missed him. She'd slept horribly the last two nights, which really ticked her off because she'd only spent one night in his arms. She shouldn't be missing him already.

She went to the sideboard and fixed herself a cup of coffee. She heard someone behind her and knew it was Adam without turning around. The spicy scent of his aftershave surrounded her and she closed her eyes, breathing deeply.

Her concentration coalesced. He reached around her for a coffee mug, his body brushing against her back, and she shifted slightly, letting her shoulder rub his chest.

"Good morning, Adam."

"Grace. Did you have a good weekend?"

She looked at him and realized that she had hurt him by ignoring him. Instead of giving her a sense of power, it made her feel small and petty. She put her cup down and took his hand, pulling him from the almost empty room. She took him down the hall into her office and shut the door.

Letting go of his wrist she stepped away from him. Even though she was in her office, the place where she always felt competent, she didn't. If this was what falling in love with a man did to her, she didn't want to be in love.

"I'm sorry," she said.

"You couldn't say that in the boardroom?" he asked, leaning back against the walnut paneled wall and watching her with that enigmatic gaze of his.

Over his shoulder was the portrait of her predecessor, the stern, matronly Marilyn Tremmel. The last Tremmel to be in charge. Grace wondered if Marilyn had ever had to deal with the problems she was facing.

"No, I couldn't. I don't want there to be any witnesses to this."

"Still trying to avoid bad publicity?" he asked.

She couldn't read his emotions in his tone or in his expression. Had she killed whatever he felt for her with her silence and distance? She still could feel him moving over her on her bed before he'd left to talk to Malcolm. She wanted him in her arms again.

"That's not it. What I feel for you is personal and no one else's business."

"What do you feel for me, Grace?" he asked. His tone begged honesty but she knew that his definition of honesty and hers were different.

He had no problem stretching the truth. There had been an article in Sunday's gossip column stating that he and she were old friends who'd been dating for a while. Not a lie exactly, but not the truth, either.

"I missed you this weekend," she said at last.

"You didn't have to."

"I know. That's what I'm trying to say. I'm not good at relationships."

"Neither am I," he said.

But she thought he was good at them. He had that knowledge of what they were supposed to be like from his *Ozzie & Harriet* upbringing. He didn't have her screwed-up relationship ruler that came from the preacher telling her that her mother left because Grace wasn't someone worth staying for.

"You had the perfect family growing up," she said.

"I thought I did, but it turned out to be a lie."

"What was a lie?"

Silence stretched. Adam blew out a deep breath.

"I'm not really a Bowen. I was adopted. All that *Father Knows Best* image that we had wasn't real."

She ached for Adam. For what he was saying. "Just because you were adopted doesn't mean that your parents didn't love you. They chose you, Adam."

"I don't know that. They never discussed my birth with me. They pretended I was theirs."

She couldn't stand not touching him so she grabbed his hand but kept at arm's length. "Maybe because they really thought you were their son."

"I've never been able to figure that out."

She wanted to wrap her arms around him and hold

him forever. But she heard voices in the outer office and knew the real world was about to intrude.

She didn't want him to realize what a mess she was inside but she needed them to be okay before the meeting. She needed to know that this thing between them was solid.

"I really am sorry. I thought it would be better to put some distance between us."

"Was it?" he asked, leaving his spot and walking toward her. More like stalking her, she thought, backing up until the desk stopped her retreat.

He kept on coming until his chest brushed her breasts and his hands came to rest on the desk on either side of her hips.

"No."

"Good."

"I don't like this, Adam, but I need you."

"That's what it's supposed to be like."

"Easy for you to say."

He tipped her face up toward his. "It's not easy for me to say, Grace. I don't like this any more than you do, but I know that until we figure out what kind of relationship we have, we can't both keep running."

"I'm not a runner." She said the words out loud but knew they were a lie. Hiding was another form of running. She'd created a life for herself based on who she'd always wanted to be. That was where her problems stemmed from with Adam.

She'd always thought he could belong to her only in her dreams. And having him in her life made her nervous.

Made her doubt the things she'd always taken for granted. The parts of herself that she'd been most sure of.

She realized that the closing of the school and loss of her job paled in comparison to living her life without Adam. And that was why her weekend had been so long and so hard. Because she wanted him by her side and she was very afraid that once the school situation was straightened out he'd be on the road again and she'd be in her hiding place all alone, with only her fantasies to keep her company.

Adam had his bags packed in his car and was ready to head to the airport when this meeting was over. He knew when to cut his losses and move on, but now he had a few doubts. He knew he was running away. He'd learned long ago that when things got too messy emotionally, he did better moving on. His assistant was already working on the final details of the basketball tournament.

Grace had given him the impression that she was serious about not wanting him in her life anymore. But today she was different. As always, she was running hot and cold. He understood that part of her because he was the same way. He left usually because it was easier than staying and dealing with people. But Grace wasn't just people and he wanted her.

He'd gone out of his way to make amends for ruining her reputation. He knew that most people wouldn't care if they had their picture in the paper, but Grace was different. She was intensely private and her reputation had always been above reproach. He knew she savored that.

But that still wasn't enough for her. She was skittish and scared. Watching him with those big wounded eyes of hers as if she were waiting for the next bad thing to happen. And his life, which, romantically, had always been fluid and carefree—safe—had been threatened by the deep need he had for her.

"I don't know what to do with you," he said, tugging her off balance and into his arms. The only time he felt like he knew what he was doing was when she was in his arms.

"Me, neither, Adam," she said, leaning forward, wrapping her arms around his waist and resting against him. He pulled her closer. He'd thought he'd never have the chance to hold her again but now he did.

He didn't want to let her go. For the first time since his parents' deaths he felt vulnerable.

After this weekend, he'd begun to understand why Viper bad-boy Stevie Taylor drank to escape. Understand how confusion and alcohol could lead to violence. Adam had wanted to put his foot through the wall or his fist through the door this weekend when he kept trying to call Grace and got no answer.

He wrapped his hand in her hair and pulled her head back. He found her mouth with his and plundered it ruthlessly, punished her with his teeth and lips and tongue for making him feel vulnerable…for leaving him.

She didn't try to pull away and after a moment the rightness of having her in his arms soothed that troubled part of him. He gentled his embrace, sucking gently at her mouth. Skimming his lips over her jaw and rocking her in his arms.

When he lifted his head her lips were wet and swollen from his kiss. Her eyes were half-closed and she was clinging to him. It made him feel complete in a way he hadn't realized he was missing until that moment.

Until he'd lived through a weekend without her. How the hell had Grace wound herself so deeply into his soul?

"Um…what was that about?" she asked.

Her hands were tracing a pattern on the small of his back under his suit jacket. He liked the feeling a lot. Okay, too much, he thought as he felt his body harden.

"Just showing you how much I missed you," he said. He could do a better job of it if she'd let him set her on her desk and push her skirt to her waist, like her story character. But he sensed that Grace wouldn't want to walk into an important meeting with damp panties and the knowledge that she'd just had an earth-shattering orgasm with one of the participants.

"I don't know that I won't retreat like that again," she said. "I mean, if something else happens like the photo. I am trying though. Can you have patience with me?"

"Yes," he said. Walking away from her wasn't going to be easy. He knew that he was going to unpack his bags and figure out a way to run his company from here in Texas. Not because it was his home, but because it was where Grace was.

"Thank you, Adam," she said, tipping her head back.

She leaned the slightest bit toward him. Watching the implicit trust she'd just given him by turning to him affected him. He refused to acknowledge it. He should have walked away.

He leaned down and brushed his lips over hers, meaning the embrace to be an apology for the rough kiss he'd just given her. She slid her hands down his chest and held on to his waist. He didn't rush her or try to intimidate her with his kiss. Instead he teased her lips with his own.

Finally she opened her mouth and tilted her head to the side, inviting him to deepen the embrace.

A knock sounded on the door and he pulled back from her. He dropped nibbling kisses under her ear and then spoke into it.

"Gracie, I think someone wants you."

"You?"

"Other than me," he said.

Awareness pulsed through him. He wanted to lead her to that leather couch in the corner of her office. But if he did, she'd never forgive him. There was a boardroom full of people waiting for them.

"Fix your lipstick. I'll meet you in the boardroom." He walked away while he could. Knowing that they'd turned a corner and not sure how to navigate the future.

He opened the door to find Malcolm there, regarding them gravely. Without a word, he led the other man away to give Grace time to compose herself. It was the least he could do.

Grace needed more than a minute to fix her lipstick. She sat down at her desk, realizing her desk blotter was crooked. She'd forgotten about the file folder with "Adam's Mistress" in it. Dammit. This time she was shredding it, Bruce or no Bruce, on the way to the meeting.

She lifted the blotter and realized the story was gone. Nothing remained, not the folder nor the pages that were in it.

She started opening drawers searching for it but she couldn't find it. Oh, God, she really didn't need to have that on the loose right now. *Why* hadn't she destroyed it already?

"Grace, the board of regents is seated and they are waiting for you." Bruce stood in her doorway, looking uncertain.

"I'm on my way," she said to Bruce.

"What are you looking for?"

"A file folder I'd tucked under my blotter. Have you seen it?"

"No, but I can ask the cleaning service. They were in last night for the bi-weekly cleaning."

"Please do," she said, forcing herself to stay calm and not panic. The file would show up and then she'd feel silly having worried about it being missing. Again.

The meeting went quickly. Malcolm and the other regents as well as the parents' representative were all surprisingly supportive of her and Adam dating. But they made it very clear that there could be no more public photos or stories about them.

Having her private life discussed was her worst kind of nightmare, but Adam was seated next to her, and he reached over and squeezed her thigh just when she thought she'd try disappearing under the table.

"We don't have a problem with you and Adam dating, we just don't want to see it in the papers again," Malcolm said for the third time.

"I've already apologized," Adam said. "I think the article in yesterday's *Dallas Morning News* more than compensated for the salaciousness of the photo and its caption."

"I agree," Sue-Ellen said. "But I see Malcolm's point. The school is at a critical stage."

"I'm aware of that. It won't happen again," Grace said. "Adam, would you please bring everyone up to speed on the plans for the celebrity basketball fundraiser?"

As everyone's attention shifted to Adam, she breathed a sigh of relief and enjoyed listening to the low rumble of his voice. Finally she understood what Dawn had meant when she'd said she'd been carried away with passion. Adam was the only man who'd made Grace forget everything but him.

The meeting adjourned and she hurried down the hall to her office while Adam lingered with the board. She searched her office, every single inch of it, and couldn't find the file folder with that story in it. She'd double-check at home but knew that it wasn't there.

The story was definitely missing again. She wondered if the same person had taken it. What did they plan to do with it?

She needed to let Adam know. How embarrassing, she thought. Just when they were moving on to having a real relationship, she was going to have to tell him she'd written an erotic story about the two of them.

There was a knock on her door and she opened it. Adam stood there. She could see Bruce behind him at his desk, checking his e-mail.

"Got a minute?" Adam asked.

Bruce didn't even glance up. She opened the door wider and let Adam in.

"That went better than I expected," she said.

"I told you to leave everything to me."

"You're taking credit for that?"

"Yes. I was your hero, Gracie. Admit it."

Her heart melted at his words. "You are definitely my hero."

"Damn straight," he said, pulling her into his arms. He kissed her while lifting her into his arms and carrying her to the desk. He set her on the edge of it.

"Now that the meeting is out of the way…"

"Yes?"

"I need you, Grace." He brought his face down to hers. His pupils were dilated and between her legs she felt him, hot and hard. "But this isn't the time or place."

The offer to stop touched her as little in life had in a long time. But she'd never experienced a tenth of this passion with other men.

"The world is waiting for us outside that door."

"I'd forgotten," she said.

"I'm glad."

She was glad, too. In ways she didn't want to comment on. But she knew in her heart, as he held her in his arms, that she'd found the home she'd always been searching for. And that it would be taken from her if she didn't find that fantasy she'd written.

Twelve

All of her nerves tightened. Everything inside her clenched and then there was the release she'd been driving toward. She shivered in the aftermath. Adam groaned her name as his own release washed over him.

She collapsed against his chest. He held her close. "I'm falling for you, Grace. I want you to be more than my mistress."

She wanted to believe him, but a part of her wasn't sure that she could ever be anything more than Adam's mistress. But with his arms around her, his body completely surrounding her, she felt the truth in his words.

Excerpt from "Adam's Mistress" by Stephanie Grace

Friday evening Adam picked up a pizza at Campisi's and drove to Grace's house. The Dallas-area pizzeria had rumored mob ties but Adam didn't care. They also had the best thin-crust pizza he'd ever eaten.

He had a bottle of prosecco in the soft-sided cooler in the back seat chilling. After the long week they'd had he thought a celebration was in order. It had also been a week since they'd made love and he wanted to commemorate that. He'd stopped by his jeweler after leaving the school this afternoon and picked up the custom bangle bracelet he'd ordered for Grace.

In two weeks, at the start of spring break, Tremmel-Bowen would host its first basketball tournament fundraiser. Registration for the coming school year was up and the financial picture wasn't as bleak as it had once seemed.

All in all Adam felt very good about the way things were going in Plano. The only wrinkle was Grace. She still hadn't said anything about the story she'd written about the two of them. He'd looked for it in her office to try to see if there were any new additions to it that he could use to make this night even more special for her, but she must have removed it.

Probably a good idea, he thought. He parked on the street in front of her house, grabbed their dinner and went up the walk to her front door.

She opened the door before he got there and smiled up at him. Her dark hair was down, curling around her shoulders. She wore a simple sleeveless sundress that fit her curves. She was the embodiment of every womanly fantasy he'd ever had and he couldn't think when he saw her.

She led him through her home and he followed her, unable to keep his eyes off her curvy body. He knew he wasn't going to make it through a meal before he had her. He put the pizza in the oven on the way by and left the prosecco in its cooler bag as she stepped out on to the patio.

Her doorbell rang and Adam groaned. "I'm never going to have you all to myself."

Grace smiled at the way he said that. He made her feel so wanted. It was a new feeling and one she planned to get used to. Though she knew it would take some time before she could really accept that he wanted her. "I'm sure it's nothing major."

She walked through the house feeling well-loved with the mild rhythm of Miles Davis' music still echoing in her mind. She was vaguely aware of Adam following her to the door.

She glanced back at him. "Are you planning to answer my door?"

"I have a gift for you out in my car. I forgot it."

"Geez, I wonder why?" she teased him. But her mind was dwelling on the fact that he had a gift for her. What was it?

"Because you clouded my mind with sex appeal." He dragged her to a stop and dropped a quick kiss on her lips.

She laughed. No one would have ever suspected her of distracting any man with sex. But that was the old

Grace. Prim and proper Grace, who'd never been confident enough to be herself with any man. The new Grace could seduce Adam into forgetting a gift. She was very proud of the changes in herself.

She was shocked to see Malcolm standing on her doorstep. He wore a suit, as if he'd come from work, but the tie was gone and his hair was disheveled as if he'd been running his hands through it.

"Good you're both here," he said, looking over her shoulder at Adam. But then he glanced out toward her street.

"Why are you here?" she asked.

"We've got a big problem."

"Another one?" She was beginning to think that Tremmel-Bowen was never going to get out of trouble. Every time they took one step forward something dragged them two steps backward.

"Yes," Malcolm said. "Can I come in?"

She stepped back, holding the door open for him. The evening air was dry and cool but she saw a sheen of sweat on Malcolm's brow. What the heck was going on?

She led the way to the living room, but none of them sat down.

Adam put his arm around her waist and tucked her up against his side. It made her feel so much better to have him there. Holding her, supporting her. It reminded her that she was no longer all alone.

"We've been careful. We haven't been out in public one time since that photo last week."

Malcolm scrutinized her before glancing up at Adam. "She hasn't been careful."

Grace's stomach fell and she dreaded what Malcolm would say next. She tried to pull away from Adam. To put some distance between them before Malcolm dropped whatever bombshell he had.

But Adam's grip was firm. The message in his embrace was clear—they were in this together. He wasn't going to run and she wasn't going to hide. But damn, it was hard to stand her ground.

"What do you mean?" she asked, her voice a thready whisper.

"A story called 'Adam's Mistress' has surfaced. The heroine's name is Grace and the couple resembles the two of you. The local media is all over it. I'm surprised they aren't camping on your door."

"Oh, my God. I don't know what to say." She wanted to run into her bedroom and close the door. Never open it up. She couldn't face Adam. Not right now.

"Grace?" Adam's voice was deep and concerned. She pulled away from him. She was going to feel like a big idiot when she told him what was going on.

"Are you okay?" Malcolm asked.

She realized she was swaying on her feet and she could see spots dancing before her eyes, but she refused to pass out. "Give me a minute."

She wanted to throw herself on her bed and start crying but that wouldn't solve anything. Who had her story? And why would they release it to the media?

"I wrote the story," she said.

"I figured," Malcolm said.

"How did it get released?" she asked, not looking at Adam. Later she'd deal with him. And telling him about her secret fantasy.

Malcolm rubbed a hand over the top of his head and then cleared his throat. "My sources said it was Dawn. But I can't figure out how she got a copy of it."

Her heart sank. She'd tried to set up some interviews for the other woman out of state. But Dawn hadn't returned any of her calls over the past week. "I printed it out at work because my home printer was out of ink. Dawn was in my office alone for a minute—she must have taken it."

"This isn't going to be easy to manage," Malcolm said.

"Let me get my people on it," Adam said. "I'll call you later and let you know what we're doing."

Malcolm agreed and left a few minutes later. Grace sank further into herself, trying to figure out how to explain the story to Adam. She risked a glance up at him.

"I bet you have a lot of questions."

"I do."

"It's going to be hard to explain."

"I'm sure it won't be that complicated. Want to go out on the patio?"

"Yes," she said, wondering why he was being so calm. If she'd heard he'd written a story about her, she'd demand answers.

"Um…I don't know where to start, except to say that

I wrote an erotic story about you and me. I was going to enter it in a writing contest but then changed my mind. I mean, I'm the headmistress at a prep school, I can't exactly publish an erotic story, even under a pseudonym."

He didn't say anything. Finally she looked at him to find him watching her with a very steady and serious gaze. "I knew about the story you wrote."

She was totally shocked and couldn't think at first. Then she thought too much and she realized when he must have seen it.

"Did you read it before you decided to help me save the school?"

"Yes."

Adam knew he'd made a mistake. From their first lunch he'd known that he'd crossed a barrier she'd find unforgivable. But the action had been taken and it was too late to go back and undo it.

"I thought you said that truth was important to you," she said, pacing away from him. But she didn't stop and face him, she kept walking around the patio.

"It is." He knew that he wasn't going to convince her with just words. He was scrambling to think of something to say or do to make this right. To fix the hurt she felt and get her to move past it. But he had no easy answers.

"What do you call reading my story…oh, my God, that's not all you did," she said. She stopped pacing to stand in front of him. Her hands were on her hips and her eyes blazed at him.

He saw her eyes widen as she recalled the first time they'd made out on his couch. She'd described something very similar in her story and he'd borrowed from it. Used her own fantasies to seduce her.

He saw a shimmer of tears in her eyes and felt like a bastard. He never should have let it go on this long.

"I can explain," he said, knowing that he really couldn't. He hadn't planned on being around long enough for the truth to come to light. He might have thought it but he'd known from the beginning that he'd be moving on.

"I don't care." She was trembling and he took a step toward her, wanting to comfort her. "Please leave."

"Grace…you're hiding again. Let's talk this out." He took another step toward her but she held her hand out to ward him off. He stopped where he was, though every instinct he had shouted for him to take her into his arms where he could soothe the hurt he'd inflicted on her.

"I'm not hiding. I'm furious. And if you don't leave I'm going to do something I might regret."

"You have a right to be angry with me."

"Stop being so calm and rational, Adam. I'm not in the mood for it."

"I'm not leaving. I made a promise to myself that I wouldn't run this time. That with you I'd stay and fight."

"Is a promise anything like the truth?"

He cursed savagely under his breath.

"I'll take that as a yes. I think we both know that you

view the truth as something that can be bent to fit your needs. I'm asking you to leave my house."

He didn't want to hurt her any more than he already had. Any other woman and he'd suspect she was being melodramatic, but with Grace he knew how hard it was for her to let anyone see the real woman. And her story had been one-hundred-percent real wants and needs.

"If I leave I'm not coming back."

"What does that mean?"

"Just that you're not the only one who feels betrayed." He didn't add that he'd betrayed himself. He didn't want to focus too clearly on himself. He'd known that staying in one place wasn't a great idea and now he had the proof. The reason he'd been waiting for to move on.

"How did I betray you?"

She stood before him almost sanctimonious in her anger and he realized that he really did feel cheated. Cheated out of all the time when he'd never noticed her. "All those years of lusting after me. All those years of pretending to be someone you weren't."

"Look what happened when I stopped pretending. This isn't exactly happily ever after," she said, starting to cry.

He closed the gap between them. He really couldn't stand to see her crying. He wrapped her in his arms, held her as close to him as he could. "It could be. You just have to forgive me for reading your fantasies."

"That's not why I'm angry," she said, her voice muffled against his chest. Her arms were held limply by her sides but she wasn't pushing him away.

"Then why are you?"

"Because I was falling for you. Because I believed you when you said that the truth really mattered. And I just found out that was a lie. How can I trust anything you've said to me?"

He had no answer for her. No way to make this right with his words or actions. "I honestly didn't know how to tell you I'd read your story."

"How did you even find it?"

"It fell off your desk. The papers spilled out and I skimmed them to make sure it wasn't my file. When I saw the word breast…well, I'm a guy, I had to read more."

She pushed out of his arms and walked away from him again. This time it felt permanent.

"That's what I was afraid of."

He didn't say anything, wanting her to continue and afraid he'd screw up even further if he tried to say something now.

"You made me believe that you noticed me as a woman because of the way I acted in the boardroom, but all the time you were interested because you thought I was some kind of repressed spinster."

"I never thought that."

She was shaking now. "It was the truth. I hadn't been on a date in more than five years, Adam. Until I walked into Tremmel-Bowen and saw you. Then I became obsessed with you."

He was kind of flattered, but knew that she'd never seen the real man when she'd been dreaming of him. "I can't be your fantasy man."

"I never asked you to be."

"You just did. I'm sorry I disappointed you, but everyone has to deal with crap like this."

"Not everyone. Just those of us who don't live charmed lives."

"Everyone," he said, getting close to her. "Just because my life looks perfect on the outside doesn't mean that it is."

She looked taken aback. She retreated again, this time turning to the edge of the patio. He wanted to make love to her again and again until she forgot to be sad and angry that her private story was now in the public domain.

"I'm sorry, you're right. I was making you into a television-perfect version of a modern Prince Charming."

He came up behind her and put his hand on her shoulder. "Don't be sorry for that. I wanted to be that guy for you. But I'm only human and I screw up and make mistakes. And unlike a television sitcom, I can't fix them in less than thirty minutes."

She wiped her tears away and wrapped her arms around her waist. "I'm not sure I'd want that anyway."

"What do you want?"

"I don't know. I need some time to think."

He could understand that. He didn't like it but he could give her the distance she needed. He gathered his stuff together.

He walked away, knowing it was a mistake but not knowing what else to do.

Thirteen

Adam knew he had this one chance to make things right for Grace. But he was scared to say what was in his heart. Scared he wouldn't have the right words to convince her that she was the only woman in the world who made him complete.

"Was there something you wanted, Adam?" she asked, sitting there behind that wide walnut desk where he'd had her.

"Yes, Gracie, there is. Marry me."

Excerpt from "Adam's Mistress" by Stephanie Grace

Grace sent in an official resignation from her job at Tremmel-Bowen in the mail on Monday. She'd spent the weekend dodging calls from reporters and local television media, both of whom had shown up about ten minutes after Adam had left.

He'd called a few times and she'd let the machine take his calls. She didn't know what to say to him. She was so embarrassed by what she'd written and by how she'd acted when she'd realized he'd known how she felt the entire time.

She wanted to cry when she thought of how he'd taken her erotic dreams and made them come true. He hadn't deserved her anger but she'd been unable to stop herself from acting out.

She'd never had a short fuse until Adam. And she knew that was only because she'd wanted to be wanted by him. Really *wanted,* not wanted because she'd aroused him.

She'd had two calls from different magazine publishers offering to publish her story. Adam was big-time news and any sensational story featuring him interested the national media.

She knew she couldn't hide in her house forever. For one thing, she was going to run out of food before too much longer. And her house was closing in around her. The place that she'd created to be her sanctuary had turned out to be a bed of thorns since Adam had left.

She saw him everywhere. Every place they'd made love. Every inch of her house seemed to be imbued with him and she felt lonelier than she'd ever felt before.

Her doorbell rang and she peaked out the small

window on the side to see who was there. Adam stood on her doorstep. He wore a pair of faded jeans and a long oxford shirt with the tails hanging out. He had on dark sunglasses and held something in his left hand.

"I can see you," he said.

She unlocked the door and opened it. He stepped inside just as the Fox 4 van pulled up at the curb. He closed her door for her, locking it.

"Thanks for letting me in."

"I couldn't let you face the media by yourself."

She still felt raw and had no idea what to say to Adam. No idea how to move past what had happened.

"I know you don't want to talk to me."

"I didn't say that."

"Yes, you did, when you let every call of mine go to voicemail. I'm not just here to talk about our relationship."

"You're not?"

"No. I'm here as an official representative of Tremmel-Bowen. We aren't going to accept your resignation. You are a viable part of the school, and this particular scandal isn't going to break the school."

"Oh, are you sure?"

"Yes. Have you been watching the news or reading the papers?"

"No. I've just been hiding out."

"Well, Dawn felt bad about what she did. She's gone to the media and told them that she wrote the story to get back at you and I for firing her."

"That's not true."

"Well, she did do it for revenge but she regretted it almost immediately."

"I wonder why?"

"She said something about owning up to the mistakes she'd made and not blaming you for her problems."

Grace was glad to hear it, but still wasn't entirely sure that she could go back to her job.

"I think you should know that Sue-Ellen and Malcolm are giving me an hour to convince you to come back."

"Really?"

"Yes. The past month has really brought us all together as a school community and everyone agreed you are part of the school. An important part."

"I don't know what to say to you. I'm still embarrassed."

He rubbed the back of his neck. "You didn't do anything to be ashamed of."

"I'm the only one who can decide that."

"Gracie, your passion and your desires were so sexy and sweet. Please don't ever think that there was anything wrong with that. Your story changed my life."

"Sexy scenarios changed your life?"

"Your sexy scenario led me to you."

She blushed at his words and stepped farther into her house. "Want to come in and sit down?"

"Not yet. I wrote something for you."

"What?"

"A short story, like the one you wrote. I figured turn-about was fair play."

He handed her a file folder. A plain manila one like she'd used. She peaked inside and saw the title of the story.

"Grace's Husband."

She was almost afraid to read the pages. But Adam was standing in her foyer and she knew she wasn't going to have another chance with him.

She took the folder into her living room and sat on her couch and read it. It was a sweet story…their story, with a happy ending. Adam was brutally honest when it came to his own faults, but glossed over her own like they didn't exist.

She realized as she got to the part where they moved into his big house and started having children that Adam wanted to stay here with her. That he saw his home and his future in her. Tears stung the back of her eyes and she looked down. How had she gotten so lucky? To find a man like Adam, a man who loved her for who she was. A man who wanted a future with her.

She looked up to see him standing over her. "I think you might be a better writer."

"I don't know about that. Did you mean this?"

"Yes," he said. He scooped her up and then sat down on the couch, cradling her in his arms. She slipped her arm around his shoulder, resting her head on his shoulder and closing her eyes.

She felt safe again. For the first time in three days she felt the knot in her stomach ease. He tangled one hand in her hair, tipping her head back for a long slow kiss.

When he lifted his head, she caught his face in her hands. "I want that story, Adam."

"Me, too, Gracie. I've been playing at living, pretending I had a full life but deep inside I knew I was running from the emptiness of the life I once believed was mine."

"What were you running from?"

"I told you about being adopted, but I hated that people saw me as something I wasn't. A real Bowen, you know."

"Oh, well, you are a real Bowen. You proved that when you worked so hard to save the school that your family established.

"Are you ready to stop running?" she asked.

"Only if you stay with me. I've found what I was looking for here, with you. I've talked to Malcolm and the board, we want you to stay on as headmistress. Together I want us to run the school and raise a new generation of Bowens."

"Are you sure, Adam?" she asked, because she couldn't believe that she'd finally have everything she'd dreamed of.

"I love you, Gracie. I've never said those words to anyone except my parents. But I know that I can't live without you."

She hugged him tight, burying her face against his shoulder. "I love you, too."

He carried her down the hall to her bedroom and

made love to her all afternoon. They made plans for the future and talked about their fantasies and dreams.

Adam promised to always make all of hers come true. And he did.

* * * * *

Look for the next sensual story in
Katherine Garbera's The Mistresses,
SIX-MONTH MISTRESS,
available in June 2007.
Only from Silhouette Desire!

Mediterranean Nights

*Join the guests and crew of Alexandra's Dream,
the newest luxury ship to set sail on the
romantic Mediterranean, as they experience
the glamorous world of cruising.*

*A new Harlequin continuity series
begins in June 2007 with
FROM RUSSIA, WITH LOVE
by Ingrid Weaver*

*Marina Artamova books a cabin on the
luxurious cruise ship Alexandra's Dream,
when she finds out that her orphaned nephew
and his adoptive father are aboard.
She's determined to be reunited with the boy…
but the romantic ambience of the ship
and her undeniable attraction to a man
she considers her enemy are about to
interfere with her quest!*

Turn the page for a sneak preview!

Piraeus, Greece

"THERE SHE IS, Stefan. *Alexandra's Dream*." David
Anderson squatted beside his new son and pointed at
the dark blue hull that towered above the pier. The
cruise ship was a majestic sight, twelve decks high and
as long as a city block. A circle of silver and gold stars,
the logo of the Liberty Cruise Line, gleamed from the
swept-back smokestack. Like some legendary sea
creature born for the water, the ship emanated power
from every sleek curve—even at rest it held the promise
of motion. "That's going to be our home for the next
ten days."

The child beside him remained silent, his cheeks
working in and out as he sucked furiously on his thumb.

Hair so blond it appeared white ruffled against his forehead in the harbor breeze. The baby-sweet scent unique to the very young mingled with the tang of the sea.

"Ship," David said. "Uh, *parakhod*."

From beneath his bangs, Stefan looked at the *Alexandra's Dream*. Although he didn't release his thumb, the corners of his mouth tightened with the beginning of a smile.

David grinned. That was Stefan's first smile this afternoon, one of only two since they had left the orphanage yesterday. It was probably because of the boat—according to the orphanage staff, the boy loved boats, which was the main reason David had decided to book this cruise. Then again, there was a strong possibility the smile could have been a reaction to David's attempt at pocket-dictionary Russian. Whatever the cause, it was a good start.

The liaison from the adoption agency had claimed that Stefan had been taught some English, but David had yet to see evidence of it. David continued to speak, positive his son would understand his tone even if he couldn't grasp the words. "This is her maiden voyage. Her first trip, just like this is our first trip, and that makes it special." He motioned toward the stage that had been set up on the pier beneath the ship's bow. "That's why everyone's celebrating."

The ship's official christening ceremony had been held the day before and had been a closed affair, with only the cruise-line executives and VIP guests invited, but the stage hadn't yet been disassembled. Banners bearing the blue and white of the Greek flag of the ship's owner, as well as the Liberty circle of stars logo, draped the edges of the platform. In the center, a group of musicians and a dance troupe dressed in traditional white folk costumes performed for the benefit of the *Alexandra's Dream*'s first passengers. Their audience was in a festive mood, snapping their fingers in time to the music while the dancers twirled and wove through their steps.

David bobbed his head to the rhythm of the mandolins. They were playing a folk tune that seemed vaguely familiar, possibly from a movie he'd seen. He hummed a few notes. "Catchy melody, isn't it?"

Stefan turned his gaze on David. His eyes were a striking shade of blue, as cool and pale as a winter horizon and far too solemn for a child not yet five. Still, the smile that hovered at the corners of his mouth persisted. He moved his head with the music, mirroring David's motion.

David gave a silent cheer at the interaction. Hopefully, this cruise would provide countless opportunities for more. "Hey, good for you," he said. "Do you like the music?"

The child's eyes sparked. He withdrew his thumb with a pop. *"Moozika!"*

"Music. Right!" David held out his hand. "Come on, let's go closer so we can watch the dancers."

Stefan grasped David's hand quickly, as if he feared it would be withdrawn. In an instant his budding smile was replaced by a look close to panic.

Did he remember the car accident that had killed his

parents? It would be a mercy if he didn't. As far as David knew, Stefan had never spoken of it to anyone. Whatever he had seen had made him run so far from the crash that the police hadn't found him until the next day. The event had traumatized him to the extent that he hadn't uttered a word until his fifth week at the orphanage. Even now he seldom talked.

David sat back on his heels and brushed the hair from Stefan's forehead. That solemn, too-old gaze locked with his, and for an instant, David felt as if he looked back in time at an image of himself thirty years ago.

He didn't need to speak the same language to understand exactly how this boy felt. He knew what it meant to be alone and powerless among strangers, trying to be brave and tough but wishing with every fiber of his being for a place to belong, to be safe, and most of all for someone to love him....

He knew in his heart he would be a good parent to Stefan. It was why he had never considered halting the adoption process after Ellie had left him. He hadn't balked when he'd learned of the recent claim by Stefan's spinster aunt, either; the absentee relative had shown up too late for her case to be considered. The adoption was meant to be. He and this child already shared a bond that went deeper than paperwork or legalities.

A seagull screeched overhead, making Stefan start and press closer to David.

"That's my boy," David murmured. He swallowed hard, struck by the simple truth of what he had just said.

That's my *boy*.

"I CAN'T BE PATIENT, RUDOLPH. I'm not going to stand by and watch my nephew get ripped from his country and his roots to live on the other side of the world."

Rudolph hissed out a slow breath. "Marina, I don't like the sound of that. What are you planning?"

"I'm going to talk some sense into this American kidnapper."

"No. Absolutely not. No offence, but diplomacy is not your strong suit."

"Diplomacy be damned. Their ship's due to sail at five o'clock."

"Then you wouldn't have an opportunity to speak with him even if his lawyer agreed to a meeting."

"I'll have ten days of opportunities, Rudolph, since I plan to be on board that ship."

* * * * *

*Follow Marina and David as they join forces
to uncover the reason behind little Stefan's
unusual silence, and the secret behind
the death of his parents....*

Look for From Russia, With Love
*by Ingrid Weaver
in stores June 2007.*

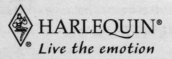

REQUEST YOUR FREE BOOKS!

2 FREE NOVELS PLUS 2 FREE GIFTS!

 Silhouette® Desire®

Passionate, Powerful, Provocative!

YES! Please send me 2 FREE Silhouette Desire® novels and my 2 FREE gifts. After receiving them, if I don't wish to receive any more books, I can return the shipping statement marked "cancel." If I don't cancel, I will receive 6 brand-new novels every month and be billed just $3.80 per book in the U.S., or $4.47 per book in Canada, plus 25¢ shipping and handling per book and applicable taxes, if any*. That's a savings of almost 15% off the cover price! I understand that accepting the 2 free books and gifts places me under no obligation to buy anything. I can always return a shipment and cancel at any time. Even if I never buy another book from Silhouette, the two free books and gifts are mine to keep forever.

225 SDN EEXJ 326 SDN EEXU

Name	(PLEASE PRINT)	
Address		Apt.
City	State/Prov.	Zip/Postal Code

Signature (if under 18, a parent or guardian must sign)

Mail to the **Silhouette Reader Service™:**
IN U.S.A.: P.O. Box 1867, Buffalo, NY 14240-1867
IN CANADA: P.O. Box 609, Fort Erie, Ontario L2A 5X3

Not valid to current Silhouette Desire subscribers.

Want to try two free books from another line?
Call 1-800-873-8635 or visit www.morefreebooks.com.

* Terms and prices subject to change without notice. NY residents add applicable sales tax. Canadian residents will be charged applicable provincial taxes and GST. This offer is limited to one order per household. All orders subject to approval. Credit or debit balances in a customer's account(s) may be offset by any other outstanding balance owed by or to the customer. Please allow 4 to 6 weeks for delivery.

Your Privacy: Silhouette is committed to protecting your privacy. Our Privacy Policy is available online at www.eHarlequin.com or upon request from the Reader Service. From time to time we make our lists of customers available to reputable firms who may have a product or service of interest to you. If you would prefer we not share your name and address, please check here. ☐

SDES07